THE INSIDE SCOUTS Help the Kind Lion

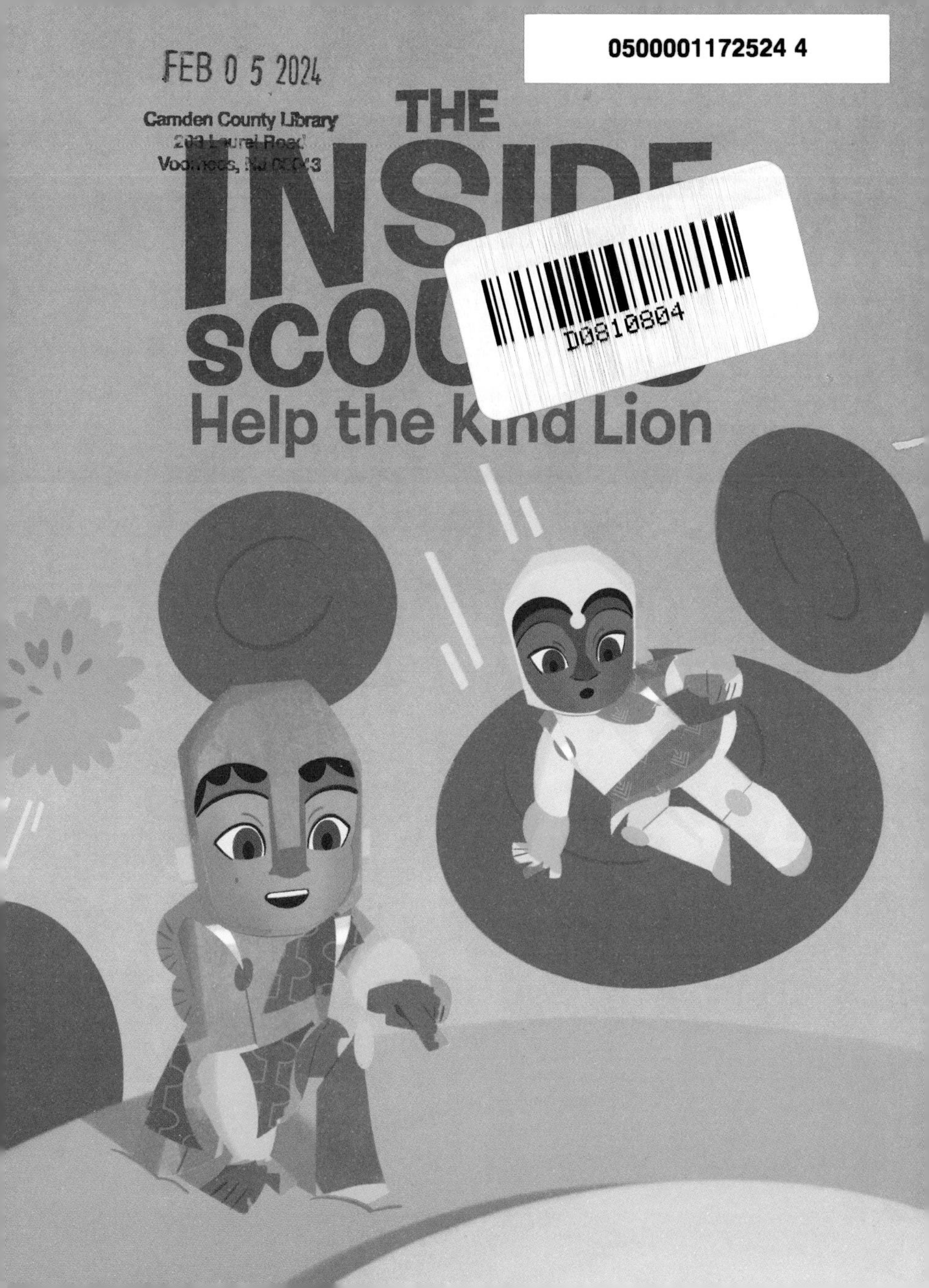

Read more adventures!

THE INSIDE SCOUTS
Help the Brave Giraffe

ACORN™

ADVENTURES INSIDE THE BODY!

Written by
Mitali Banerjee Ruths

Art by
Francesca Mahaney

■SCHOLASTIC

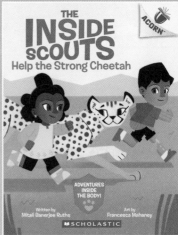

THE INSIDE SCOUTS
Help the Strong Cheetah

ACORN™

ADVENTURES INSIDE THE BODY!

Written by
Mitali Banerjee Ruths

Art by
Francesca Mahaney

■SCHOLASTIC

THE
INSIDE
SCOUTS
Help the Kind Lion

Written by
Mitali Banerjee Ruths

Art by
Francesca Mahaney

ACORN™
SCHOLASTIC INC.

To my dearest treasures, Sonya, Leena, and Jubby —MBR
To Mama, Papa, and Kuya —FM

**Thank you to Megan SooHoo, MD,
for sharing her expertise on cardiology for this book.**

Library of Congress Cataloging-in-Publication Data

Names: Ruths, Mitali Banerjee, author. | Mahaney, Francesca, illustrator.
Title: Help the kind lion / written by Mitali Banerjee Ruths ; illustrated by Francesca Mahaney.
Description: First edition. | New York : Acorn/Scholastic, Inc., 2024. |
Series: The inside scouts ; 1 | Audience: Ages 5–7. | Audience: Grades K–2.
| Summary: The Inside Scouts Viv and Sanjay use their ability to shrink
themselves to find and fix Ruslan the lion's leaky heart valve.
Identifiers: LCCN 2022036895 (print) |
ISBN 9781338894981 (paperback) | ISBN 9781338894998 (library binding)
Subjects: LCSH: Heart valves—Abnormalities—Juvenile fiction. |
Heart—Anatomy—Juvenile fiction. | Lion—Juvenile fiction. |
Anatomy—Juvenile fiction. | Science fiction. | CYAC: Lion—Fiction. |
Heart—Anatomy—Fiction. | Ability—Fiction. | Science fiction. | LCGFT: Science fiction.
Classification: LCC PZ7.1.R9 Ki 2024 (print) | DDC [Fic]—dc23
LC record available at https://lccn.loc.gov/2022036895

10 9 8 7 6 5 4 3 2 1   24 25 26 27 28
Printed in India 197

First edition, February 2024
Edited by Katie Carella
Book design by Maria Mercado

Table of Contents

Meet the Inside Scouts

They have the power to shrink super small.
They go inside animals to help them feel better.

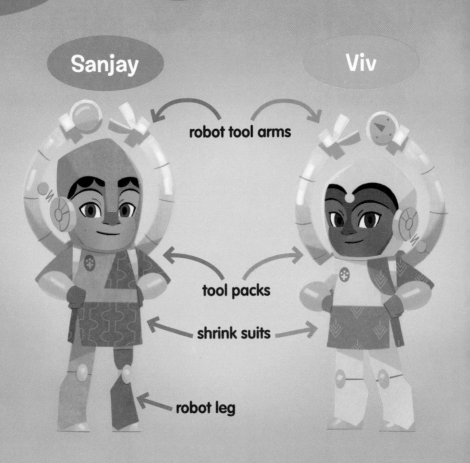

Sanjay

Viv

robot tool arms

tool packs

shrink suits

robot leg

Where Is the Leak?

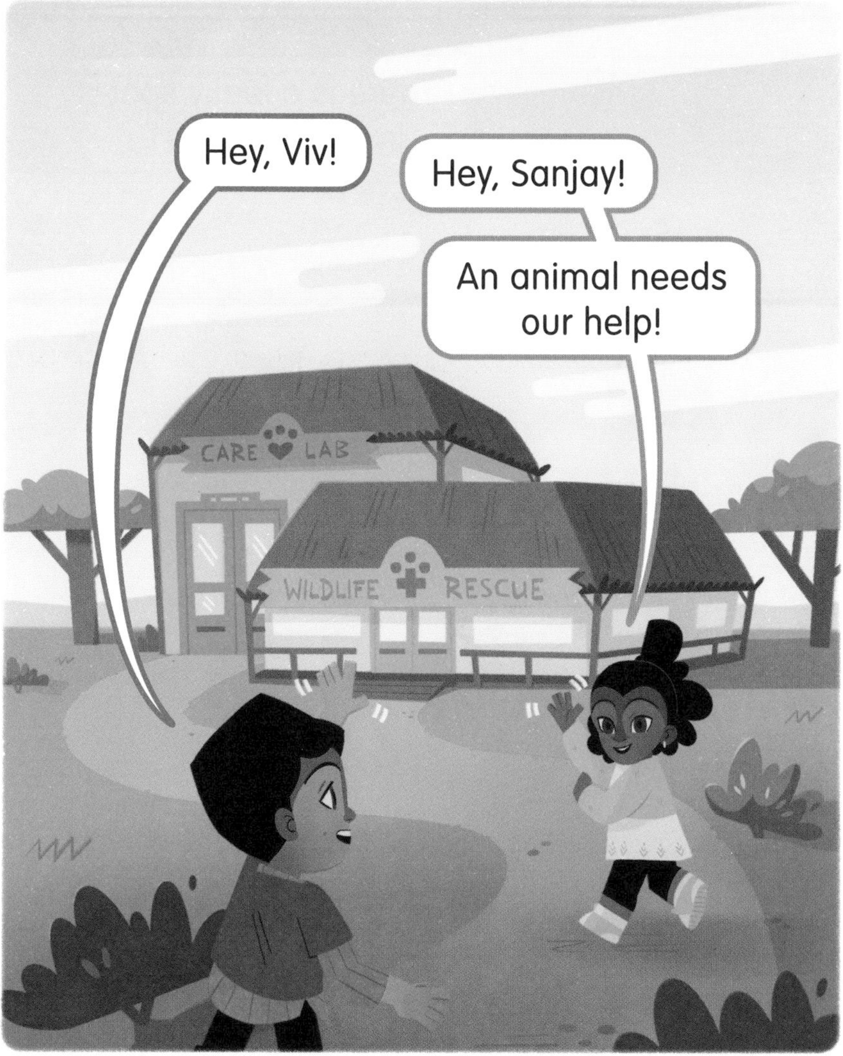
Hey, Viv!
Hey, Sanjay!
An animal needs our help!
CARE LAB
WILDLIFE RESCUE

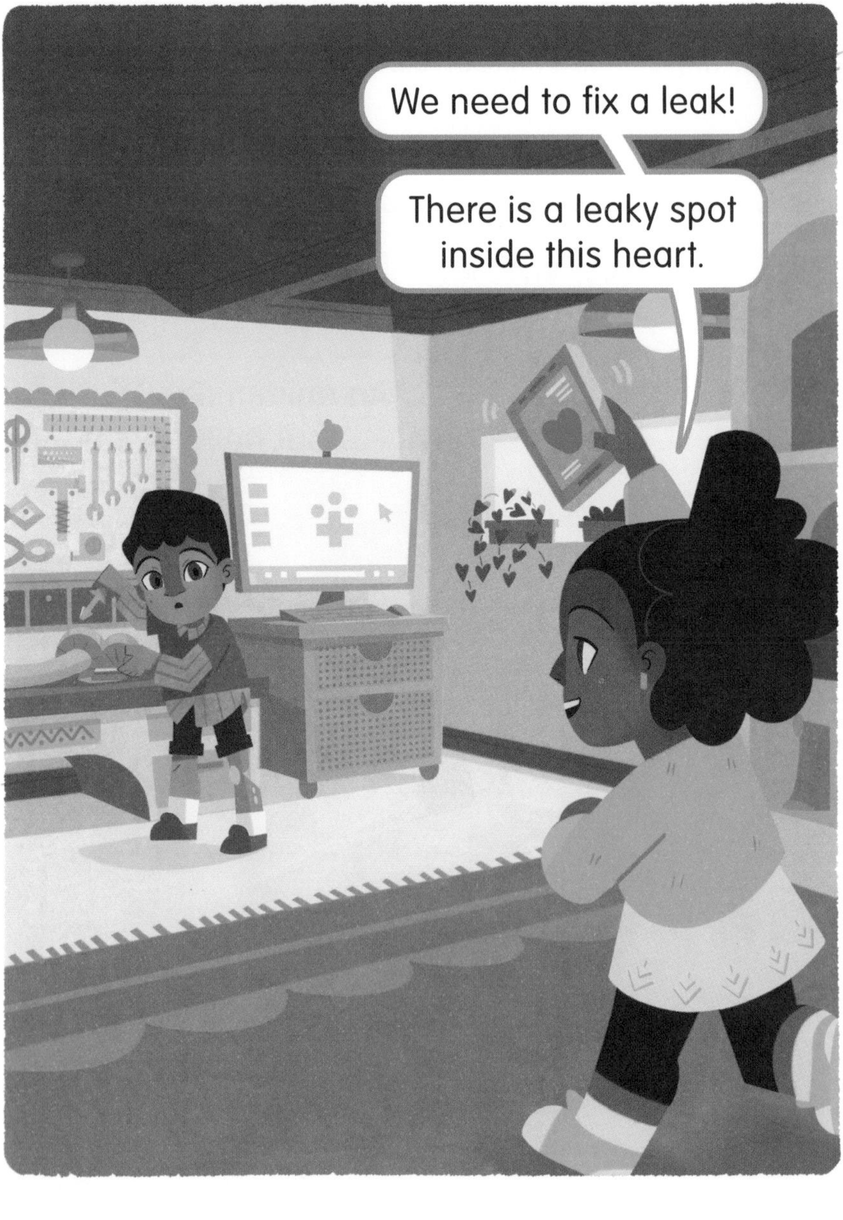
We need to fix a leak!
There is a leaky spot inside this heart.

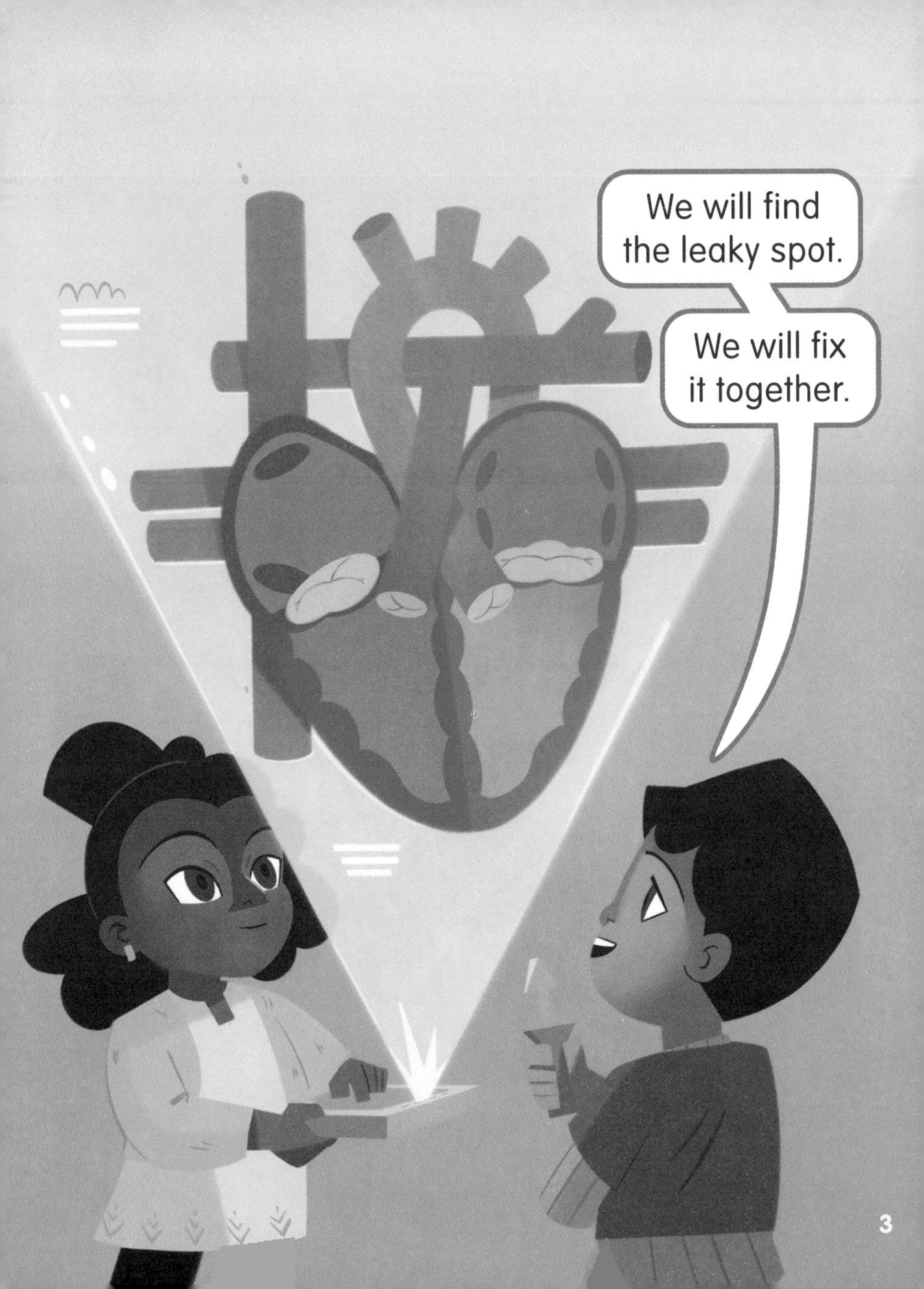
We will find the leaky spot.
We will fix it together.

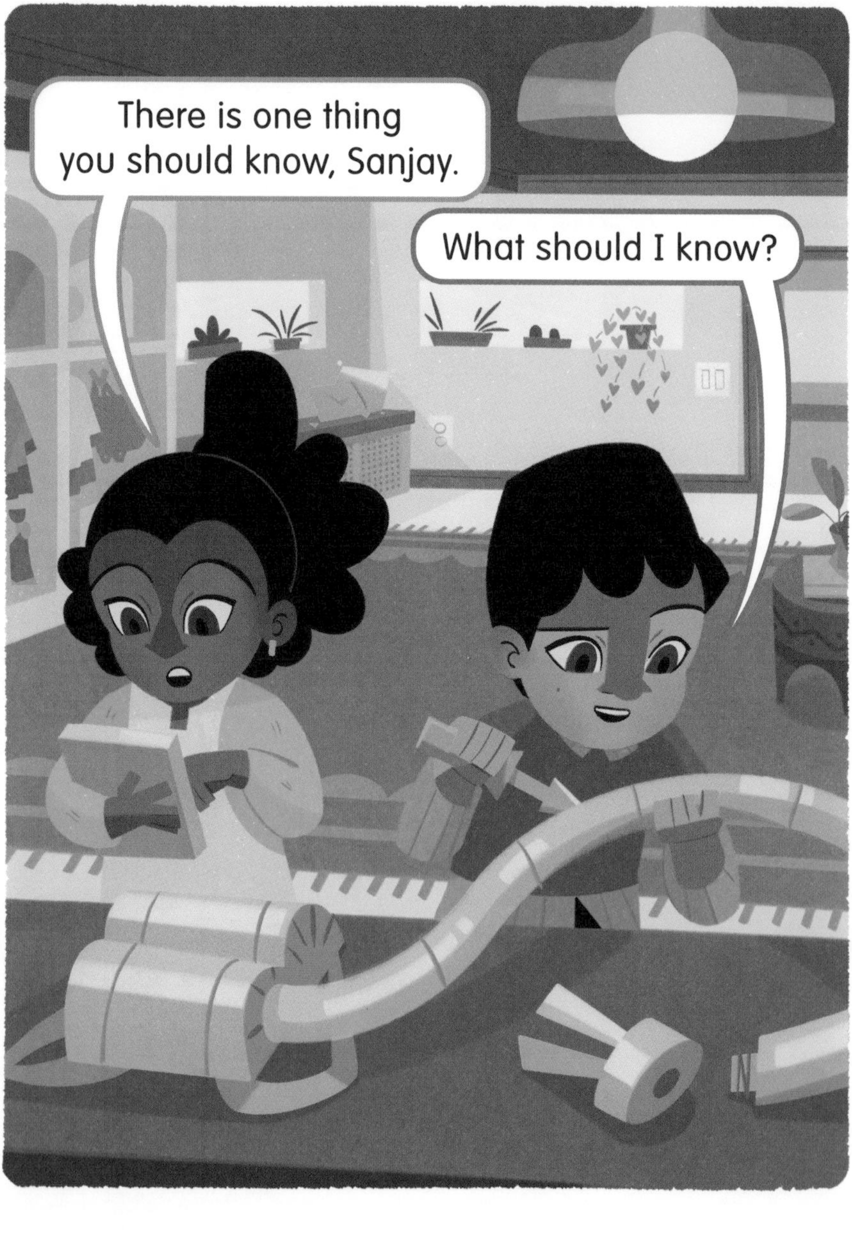
There is one thing you should know, Sanjay.
What should I know?

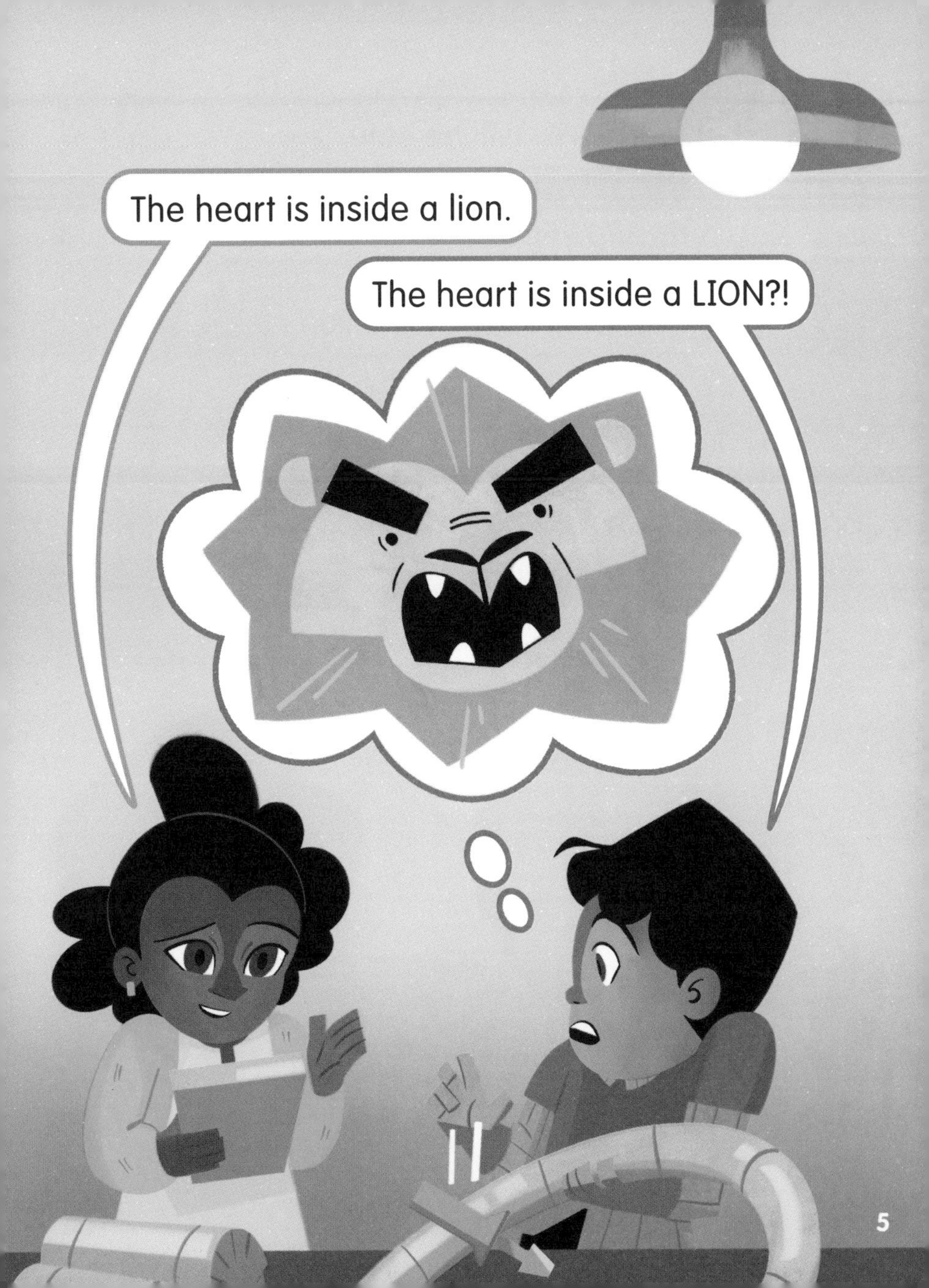
The heart is inside a lion.
The heart is inside a LION?!

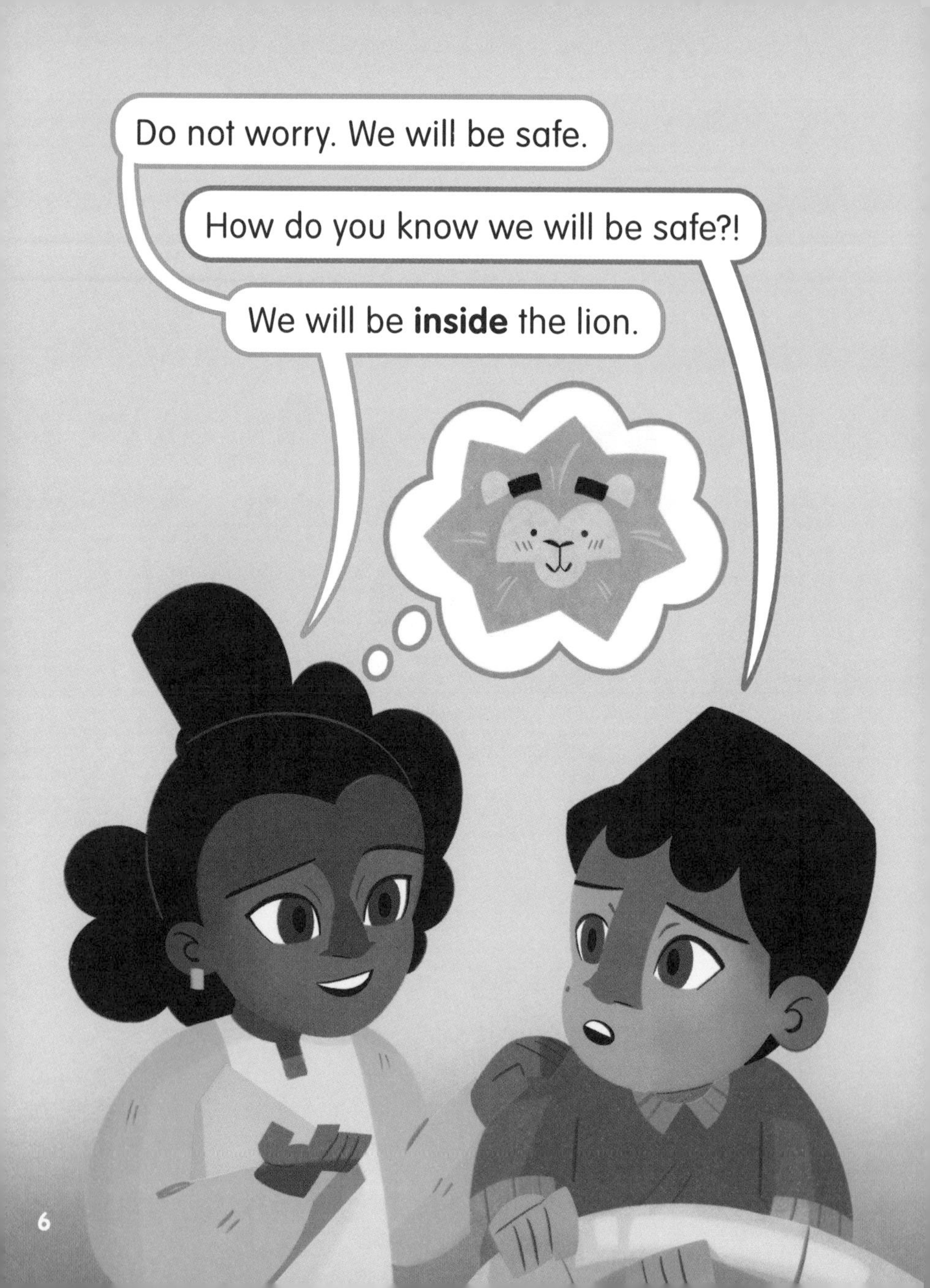
Do not worry. We will be safe.
How do you know we will be safe?!
We will be **inside** the lion.

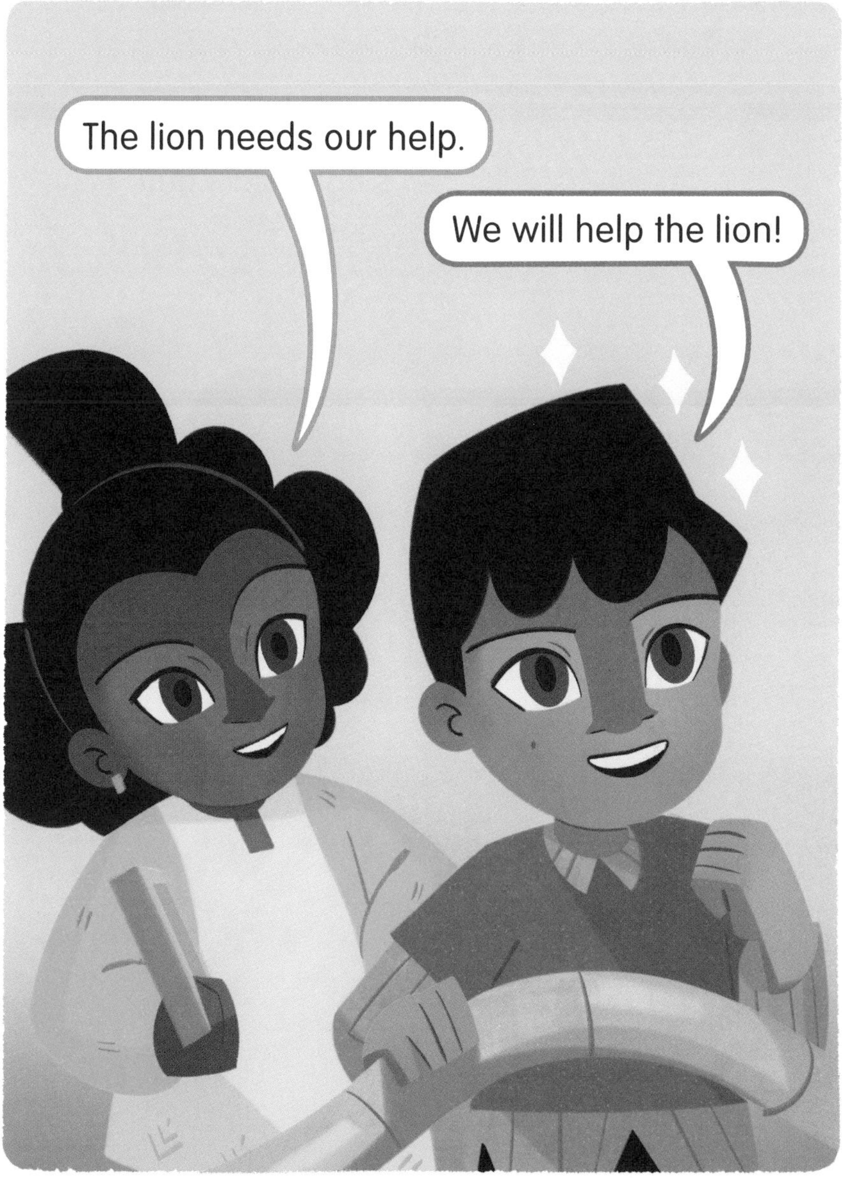
The lion needs our help.
We will help the lion!

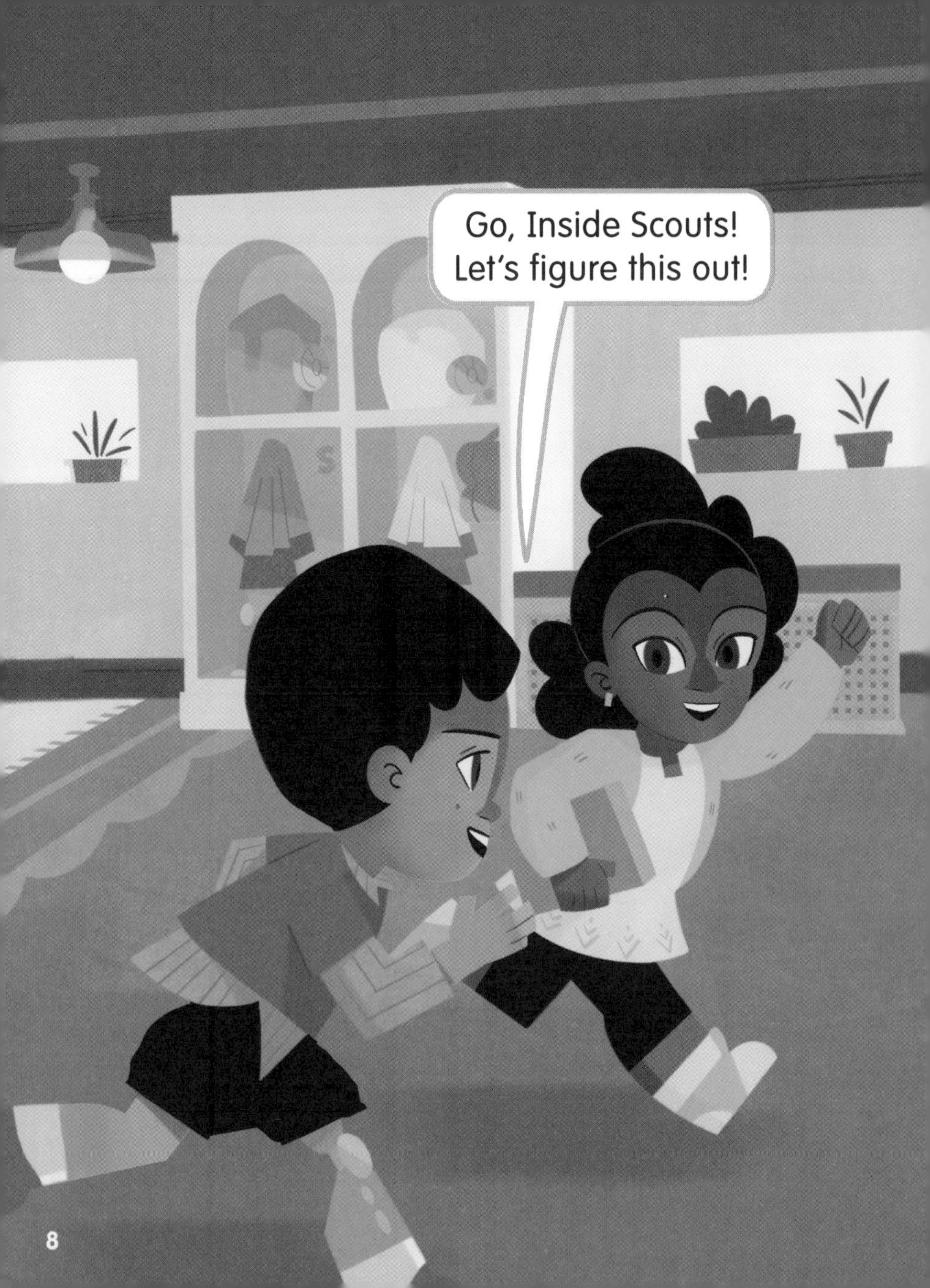
Go, Inside Scouts!
Let's figure this out!

I Want to Run!

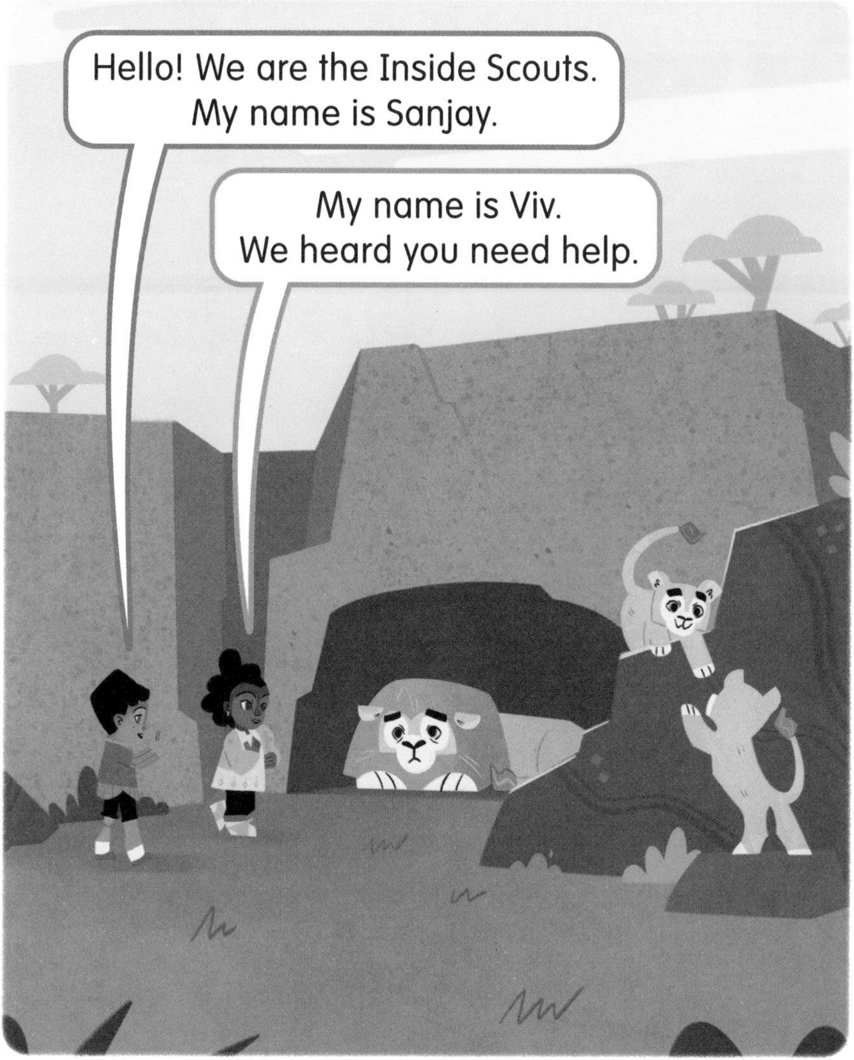
Hello! We are the Inside Scouts.
My name is Sanjay.
My name is Viv.
We heard you need help.

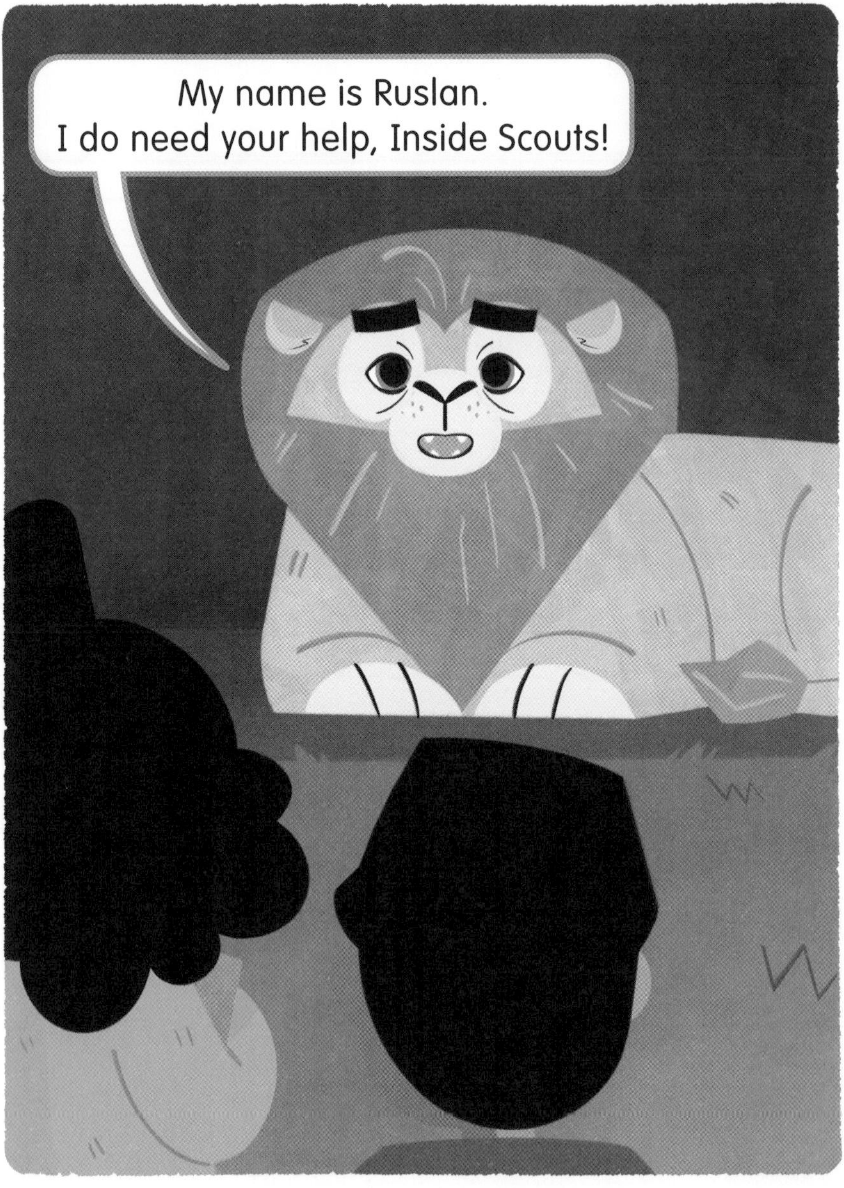
My name is Ruslan.
I do need your help, Inside Scouts!

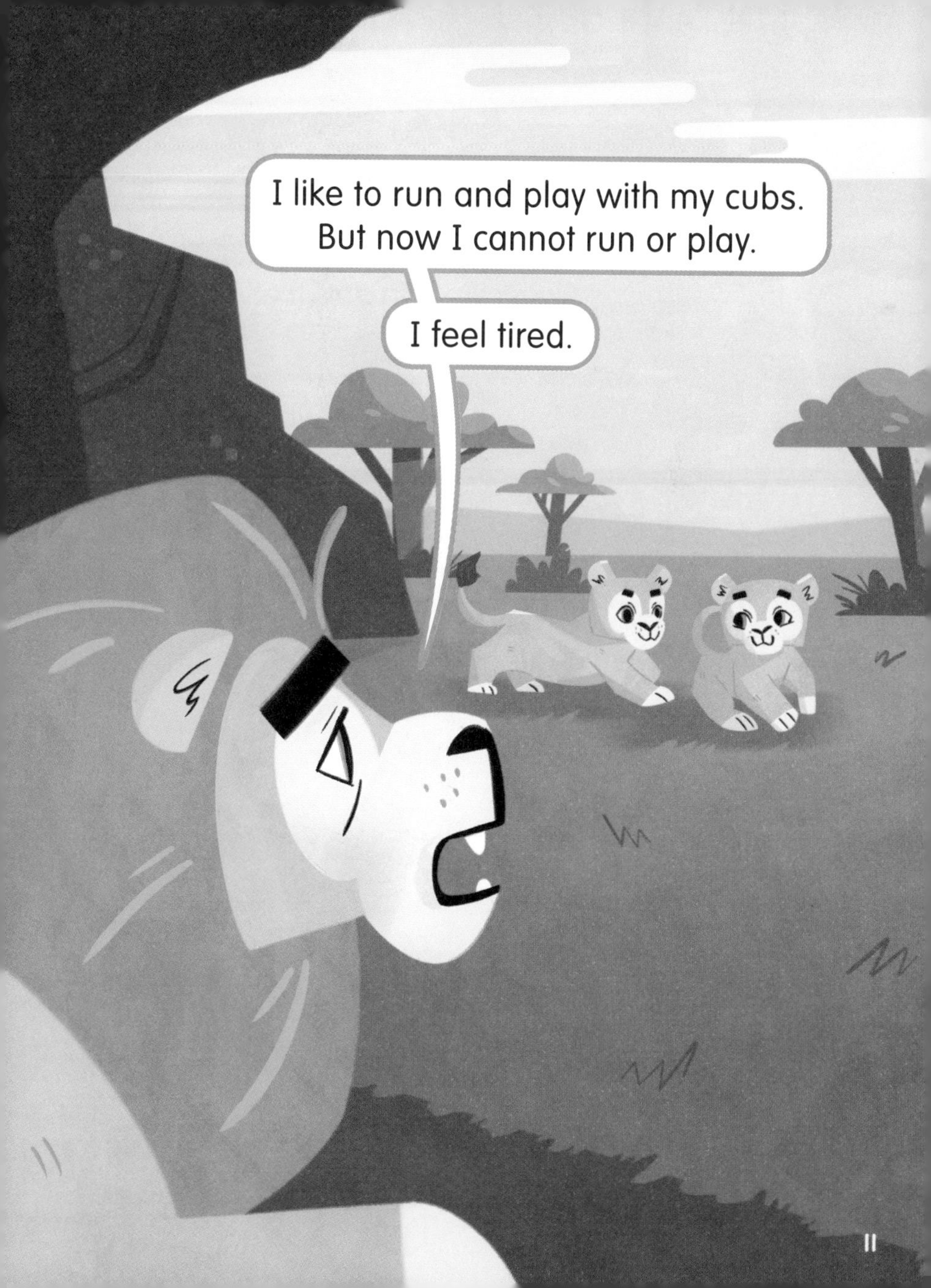
I like to run and play with my cubs. But now I cannot run or play.
I feel tired.

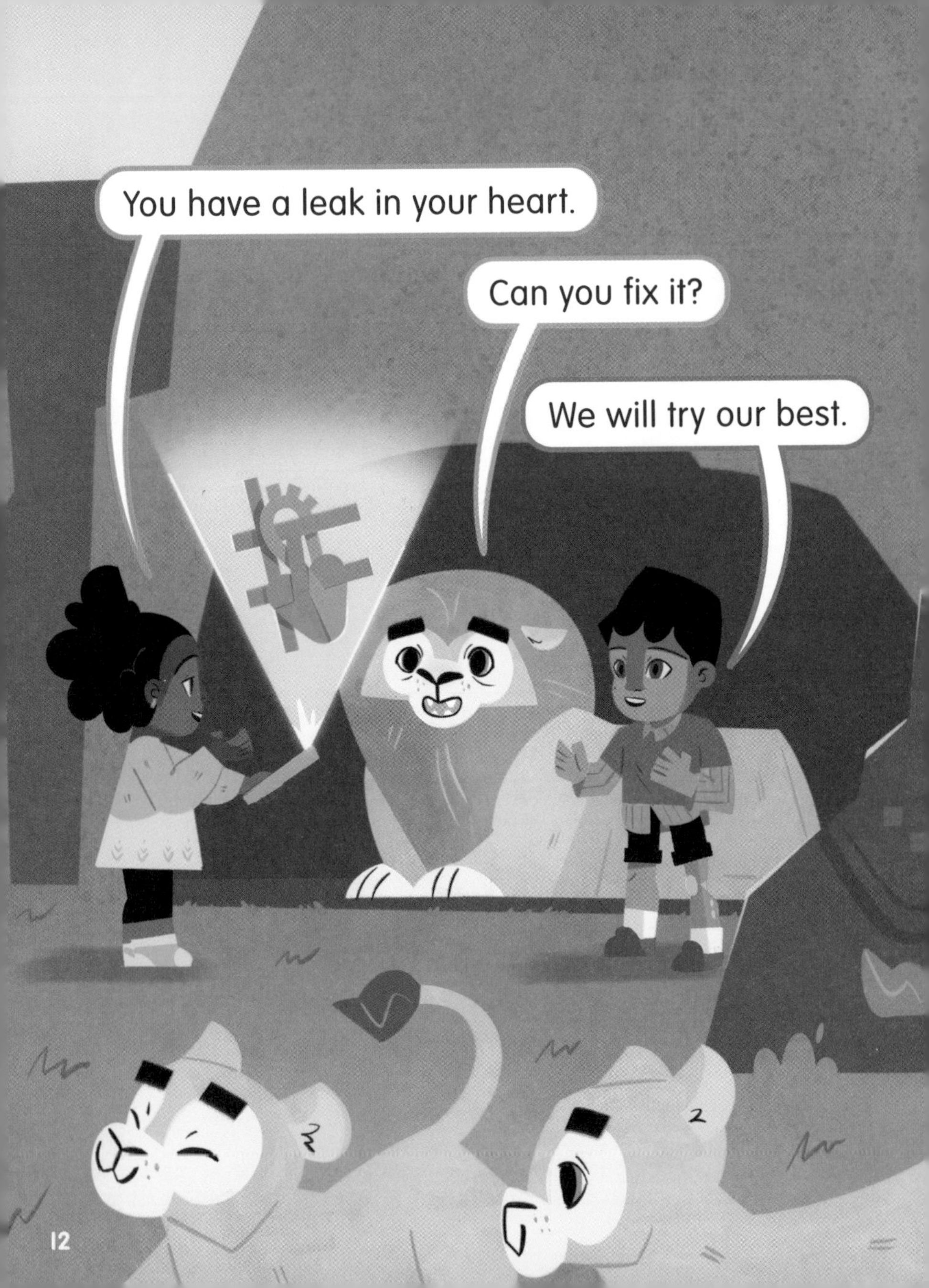
You have a leak in your heart.
Can you fix it?
We will try our best.

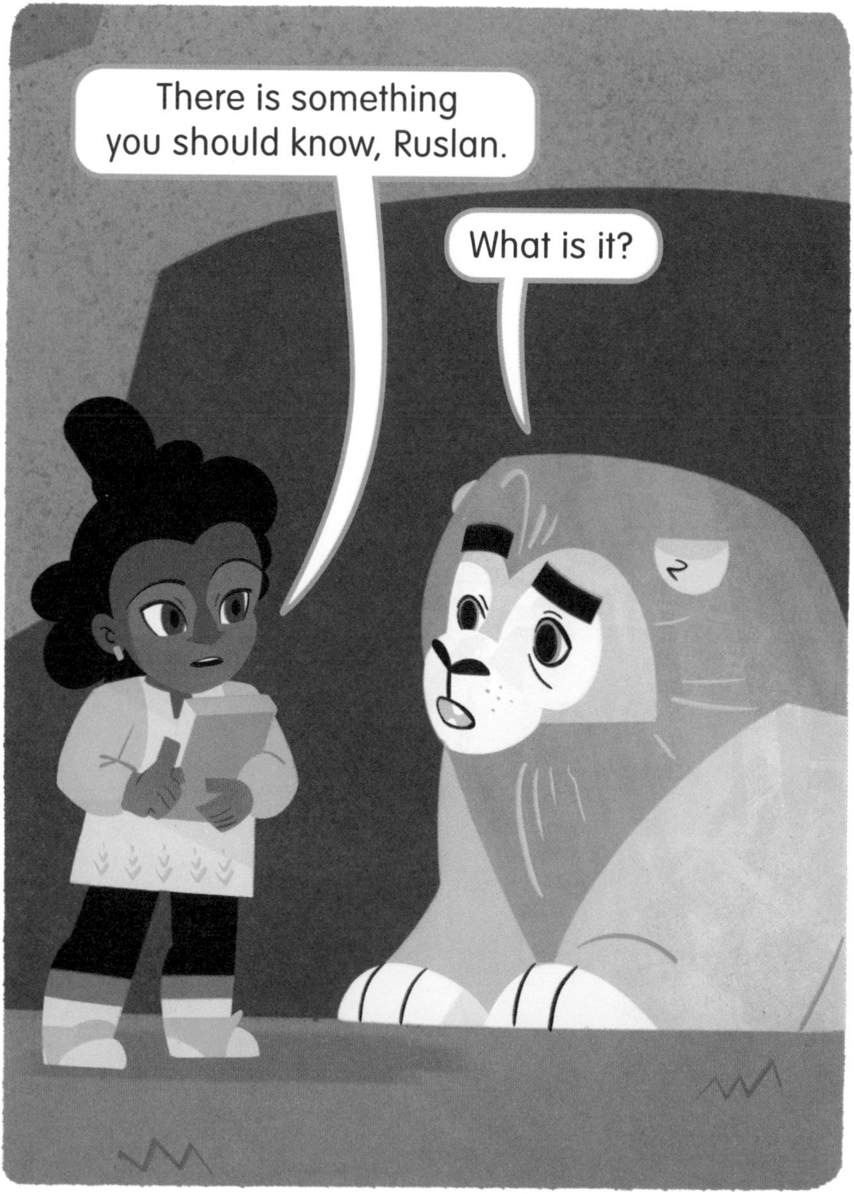
There is something you should know, Ruslan.
What is it?

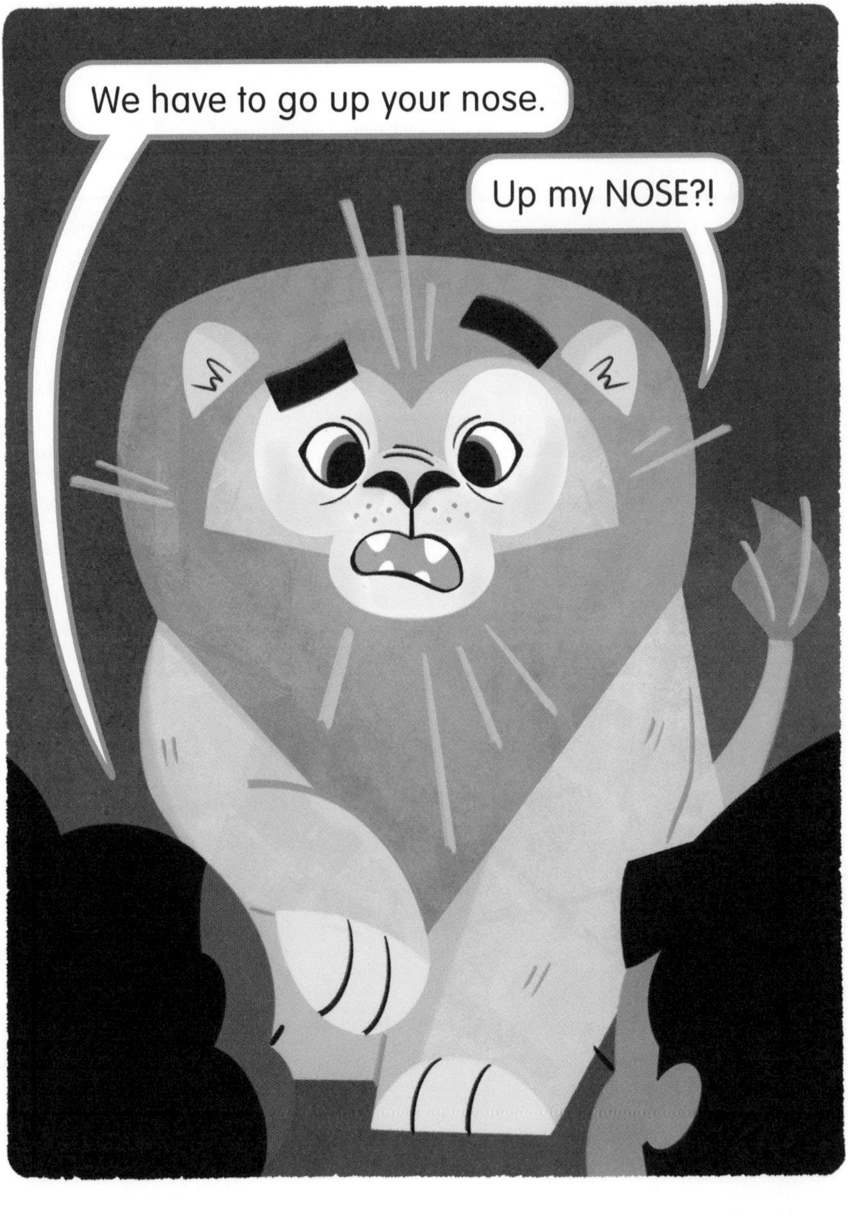
We have to go up your nose.
Up my NOSE?!

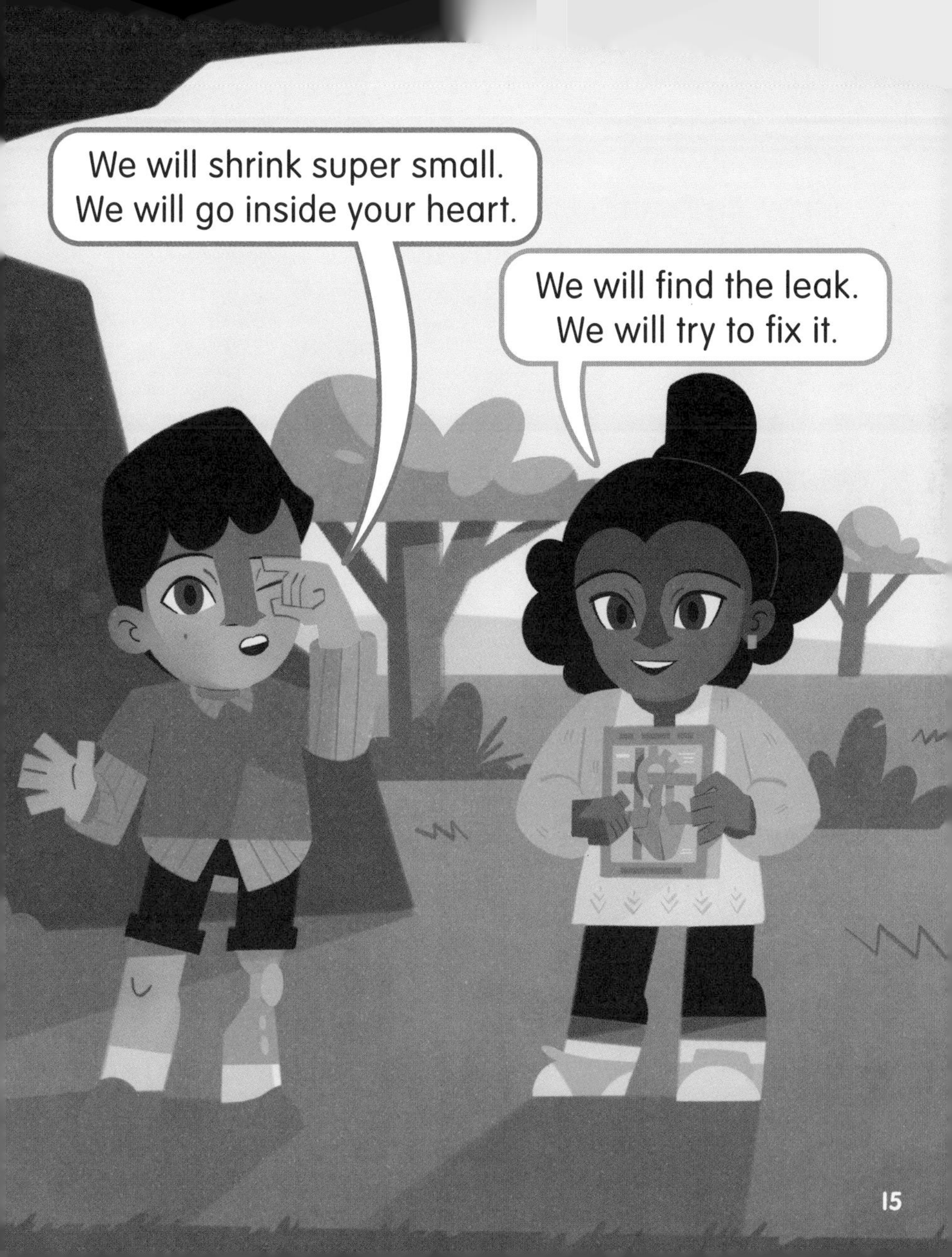
We will shrink super small. We will go inside your heart.
We will find the leak. We will try to fix it.

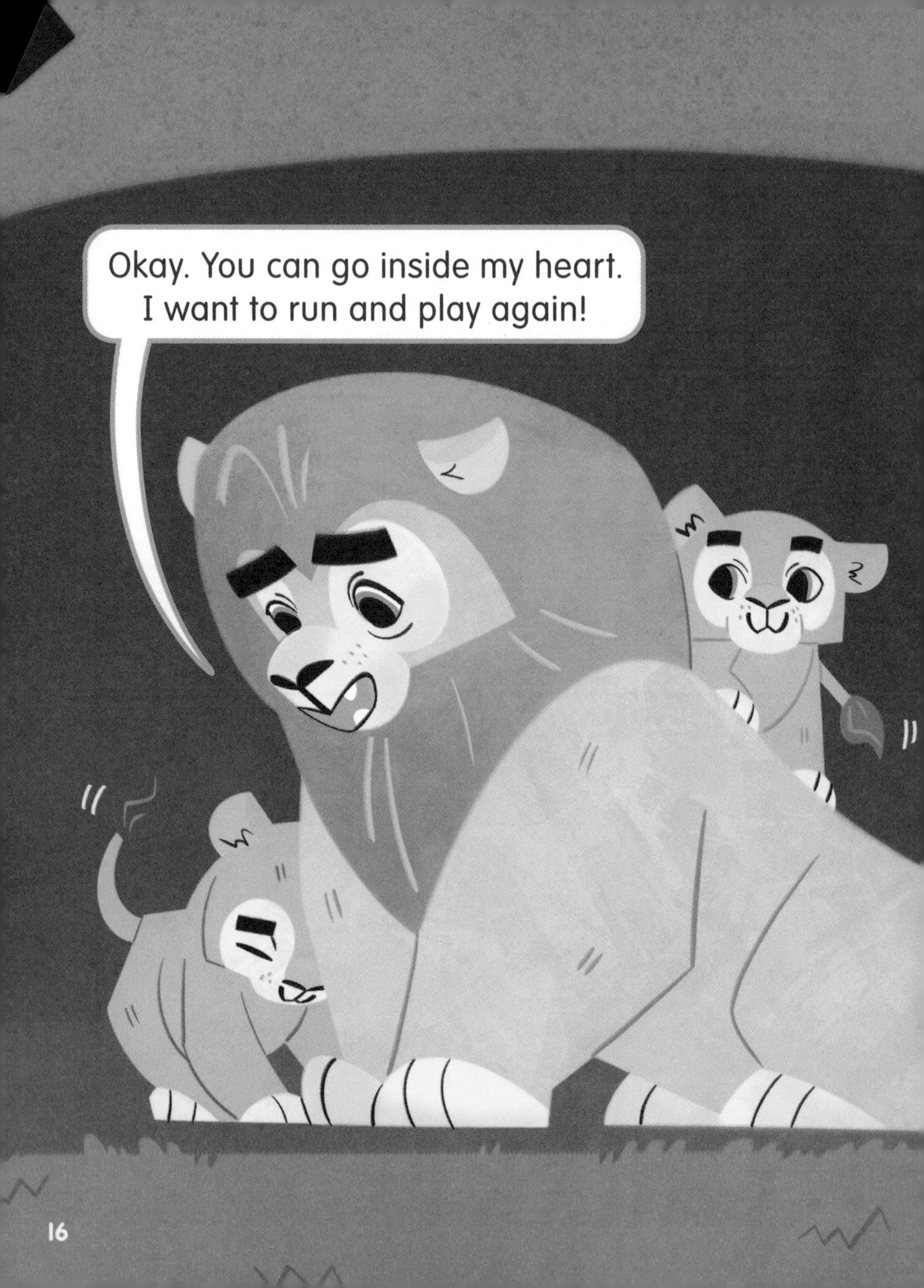
Okay. You can go inside my heart.
I want to run and play again!

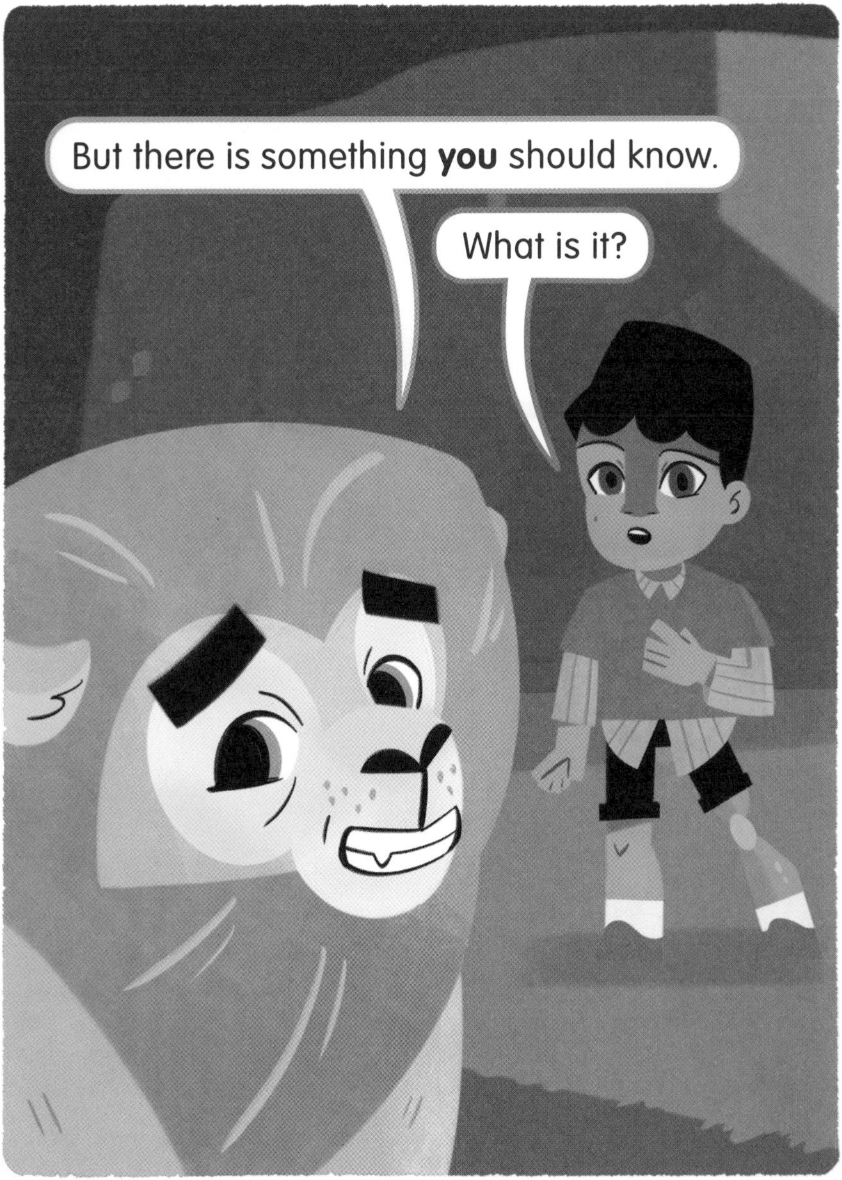
But there is something **you** should know.
What is it?

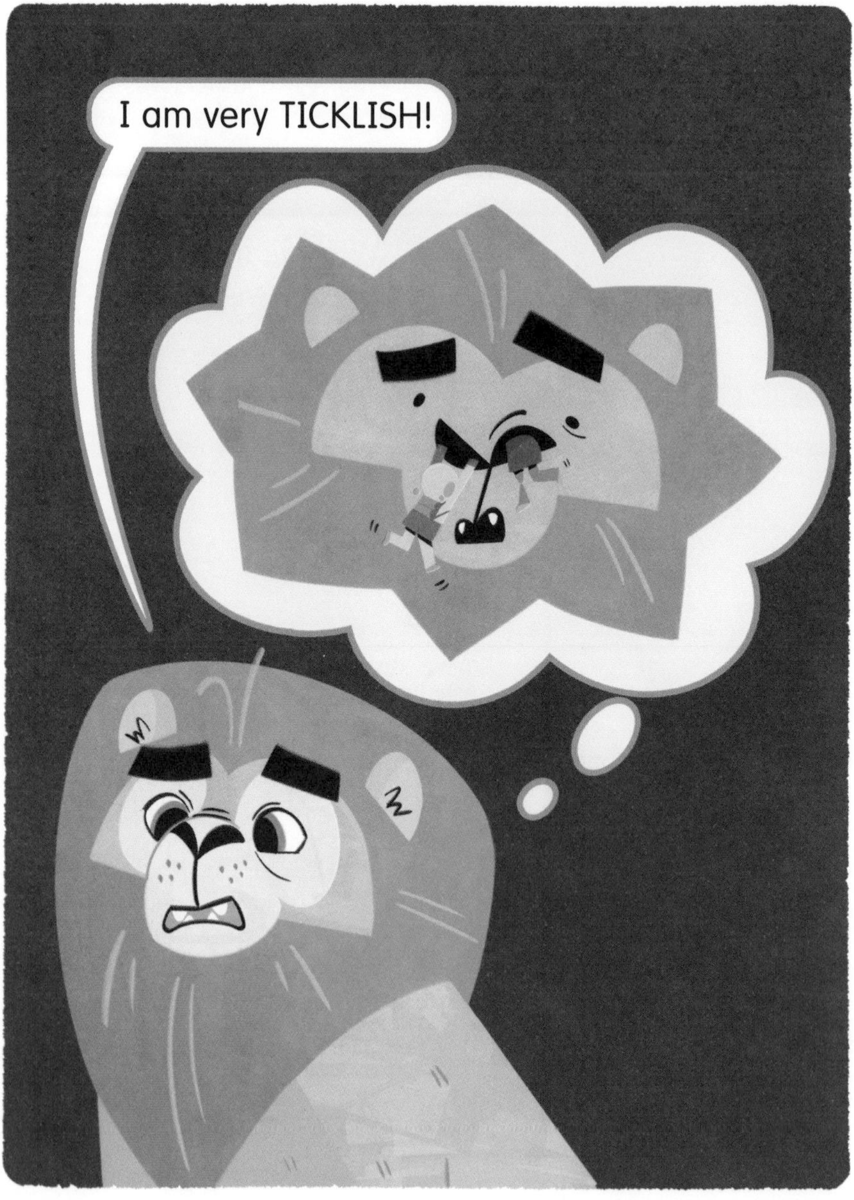
I am very TICKLISH!

We Are Ready!

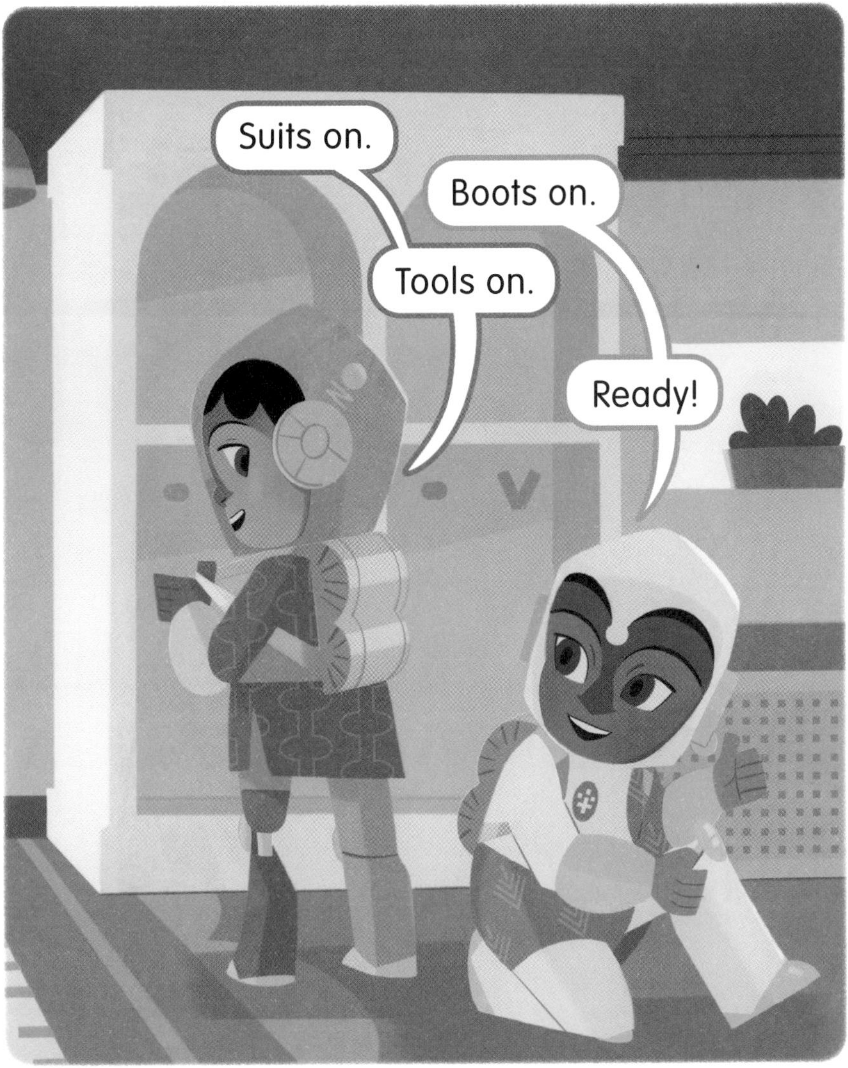
Suits on.
Boots on.
Tools on.
Ready!

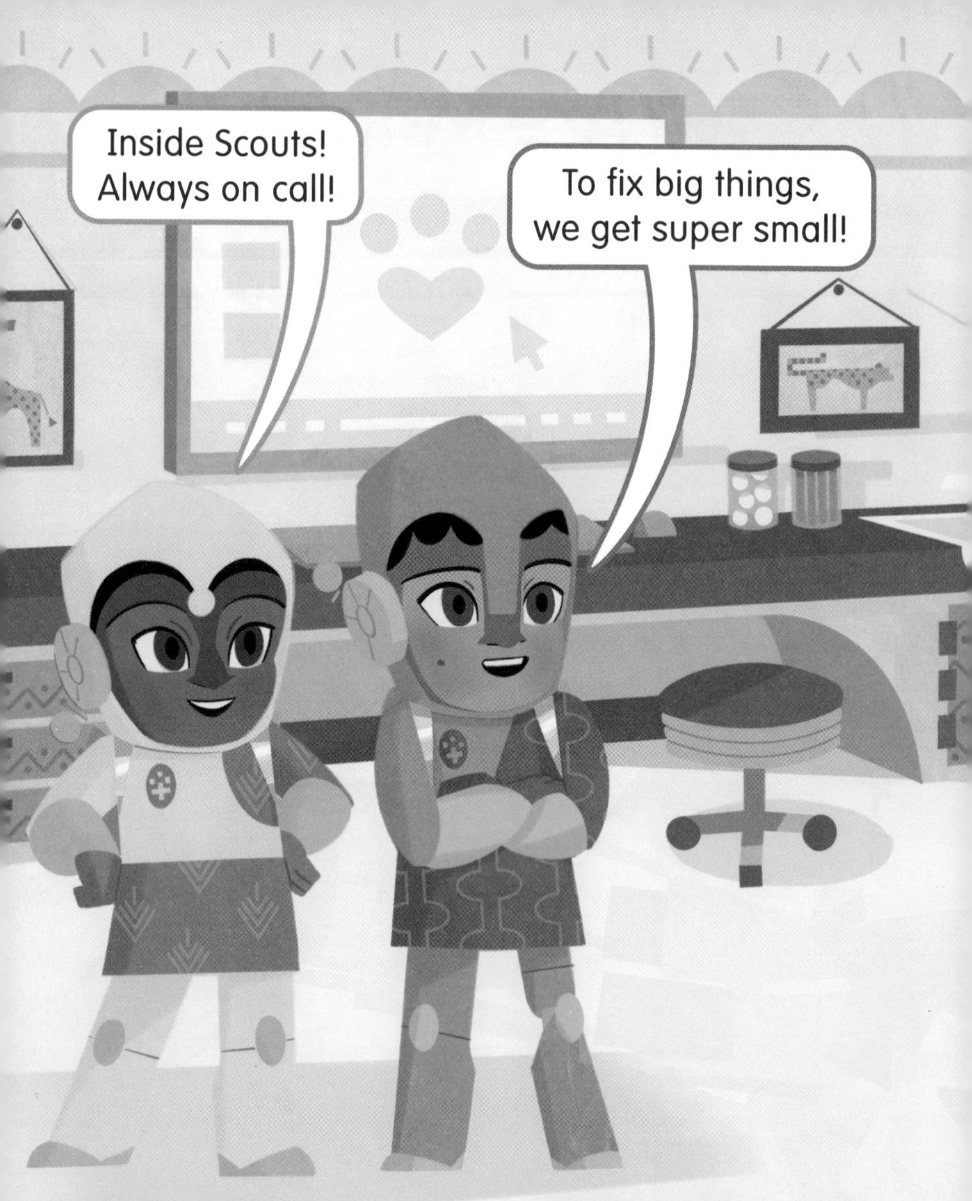
Inside Scouts! Always on call!
To fix big things, we get super small!

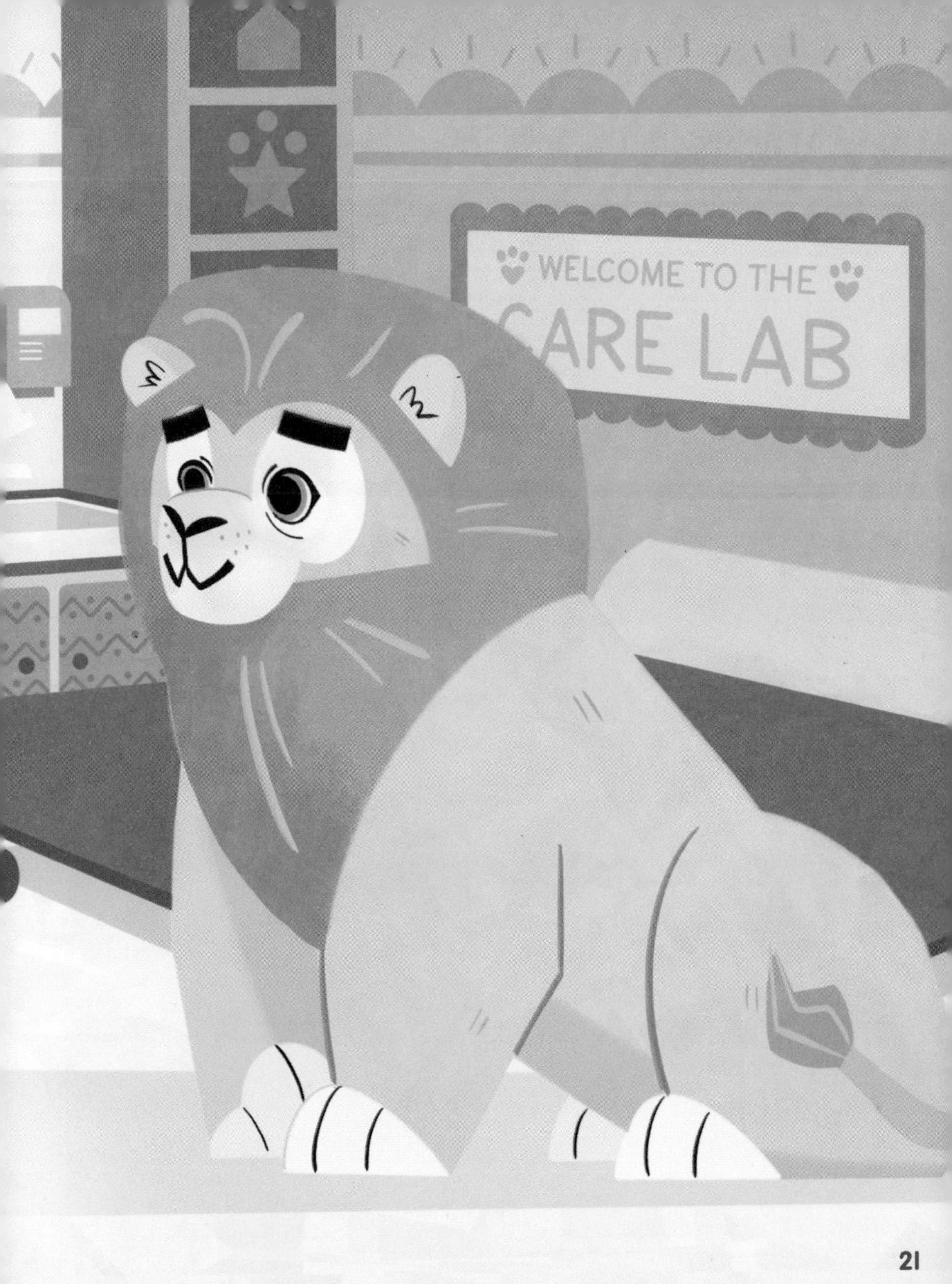
WELCOME TO THE
CARE LAB

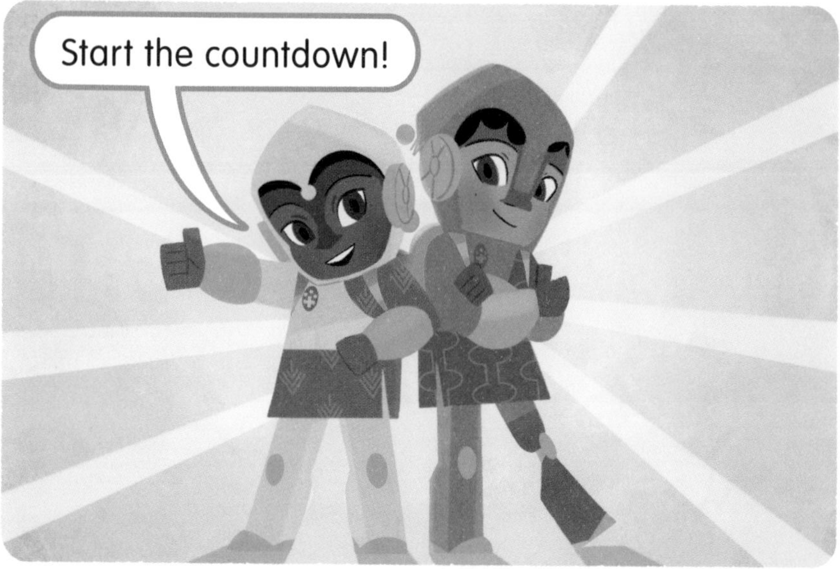
Start the countdown!

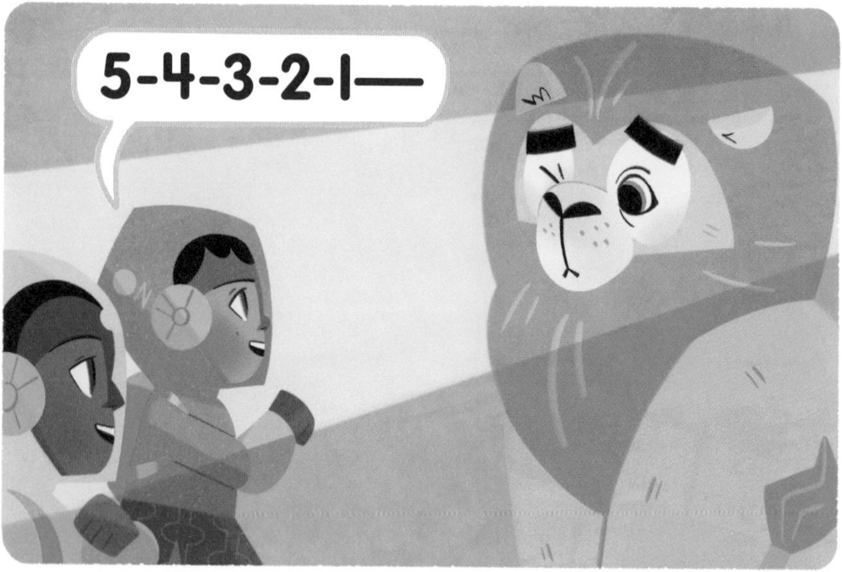
5-4-3-2-1—

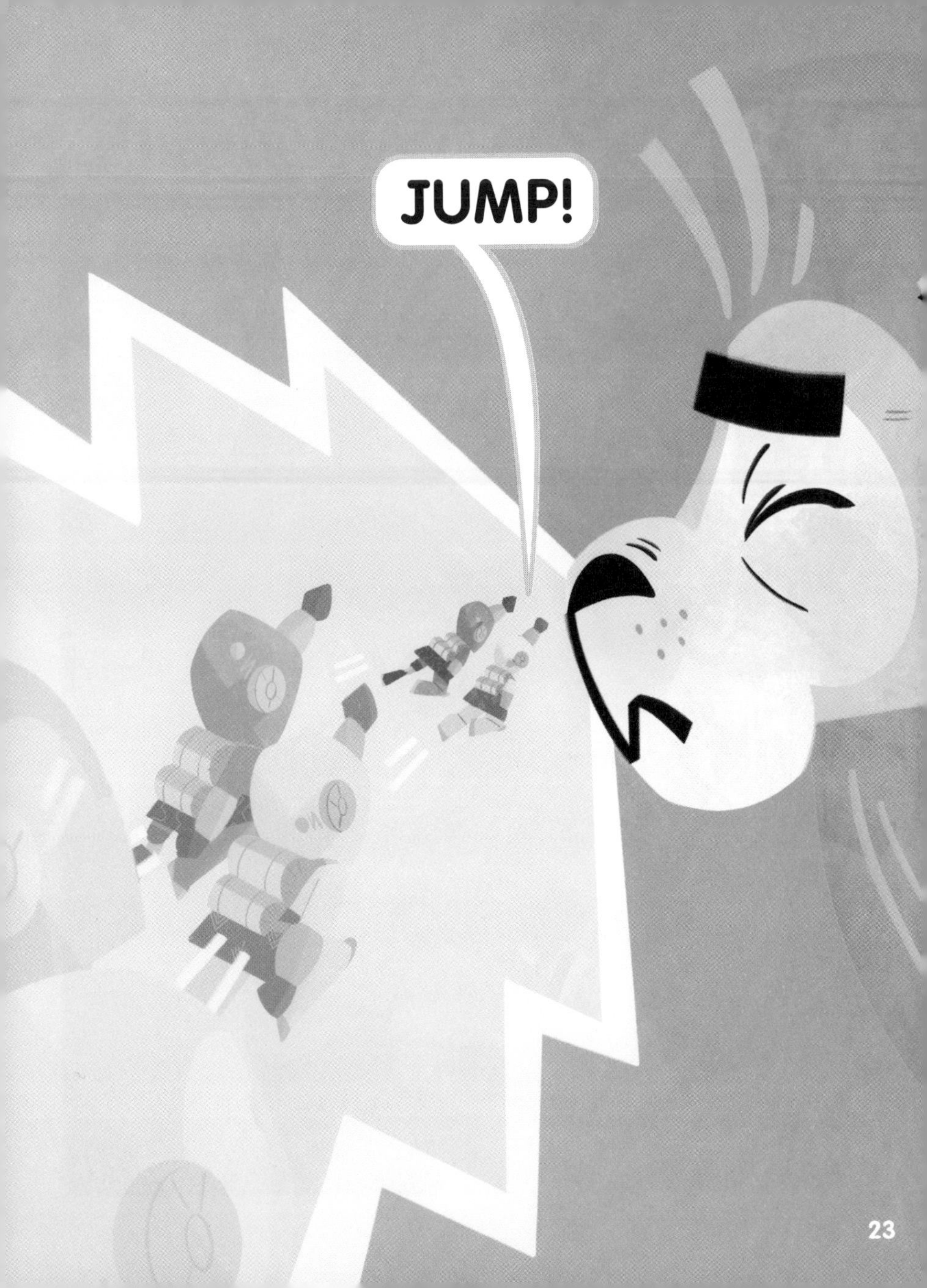
JUMP!

We Find the Problem

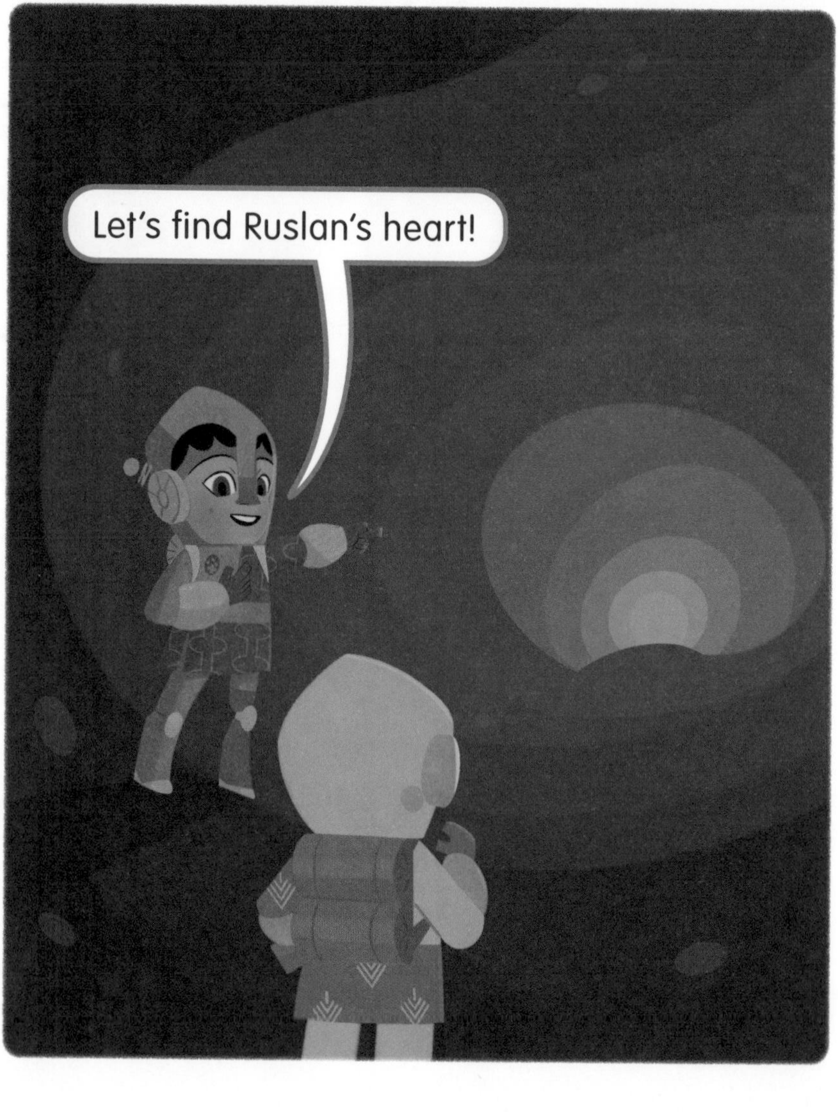
Let's find Ruslan's heart!

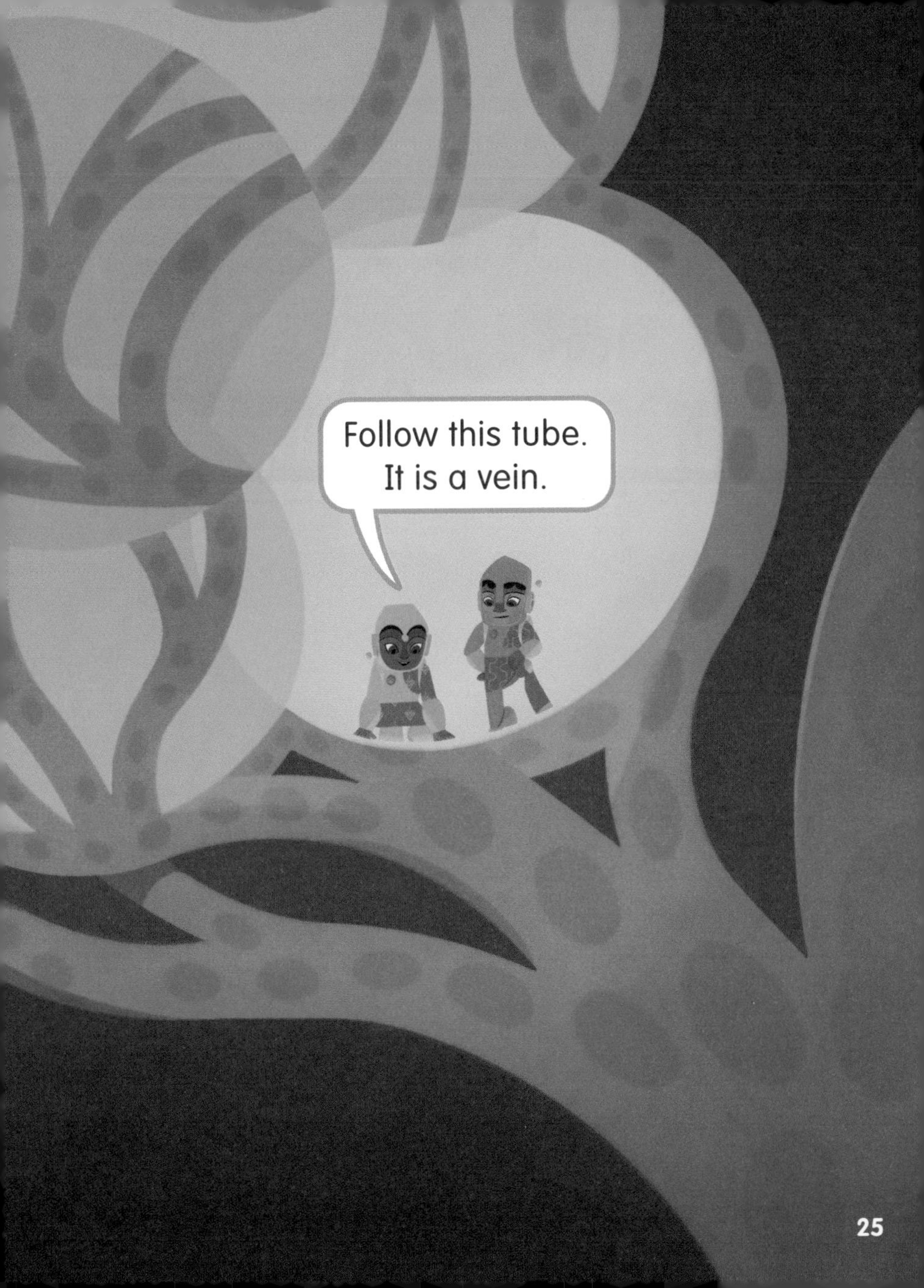
Follow this tube.
It is a vein.

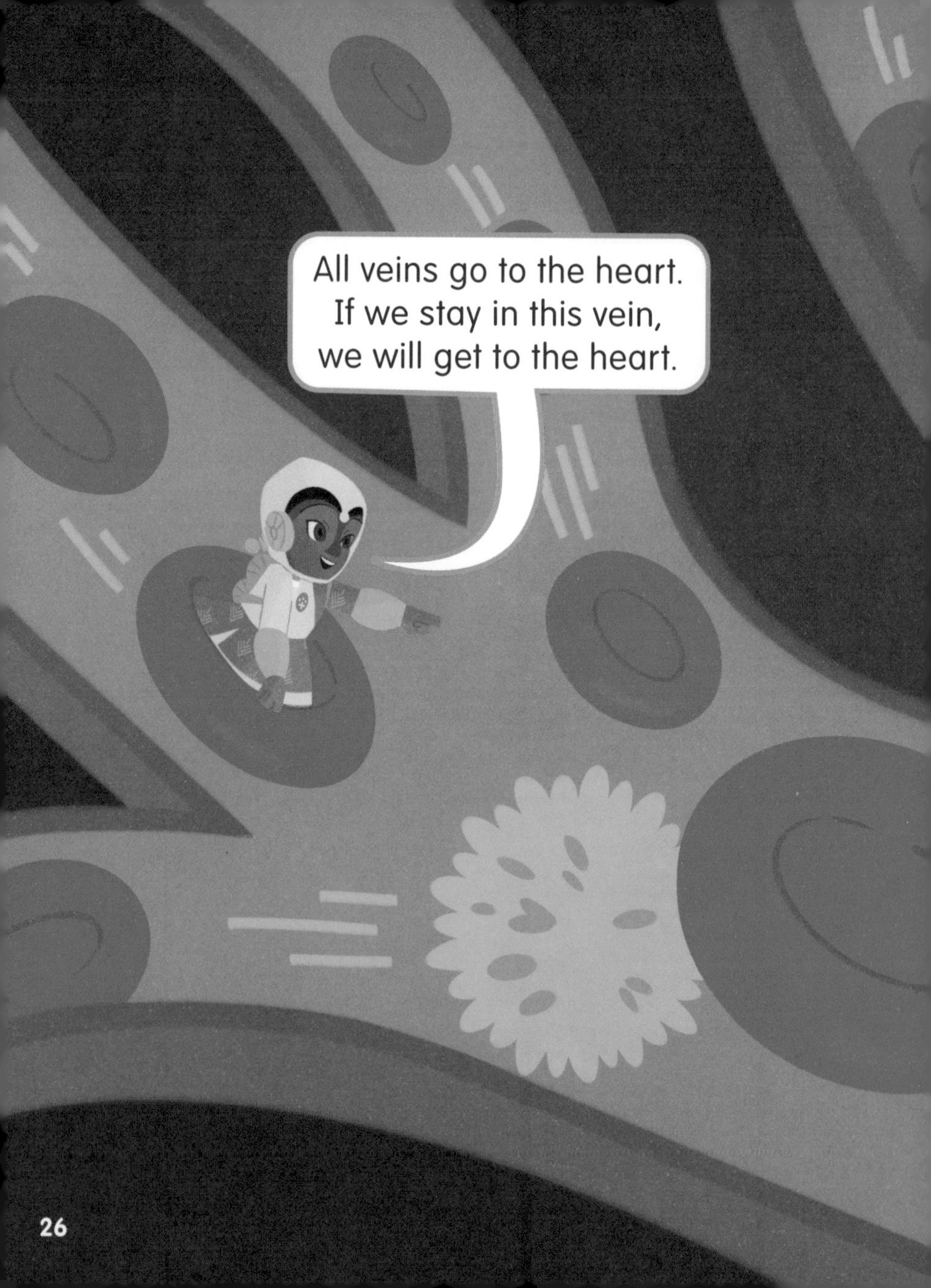
All veins go to the heart. If we stay in this vein, we will get to the heart.

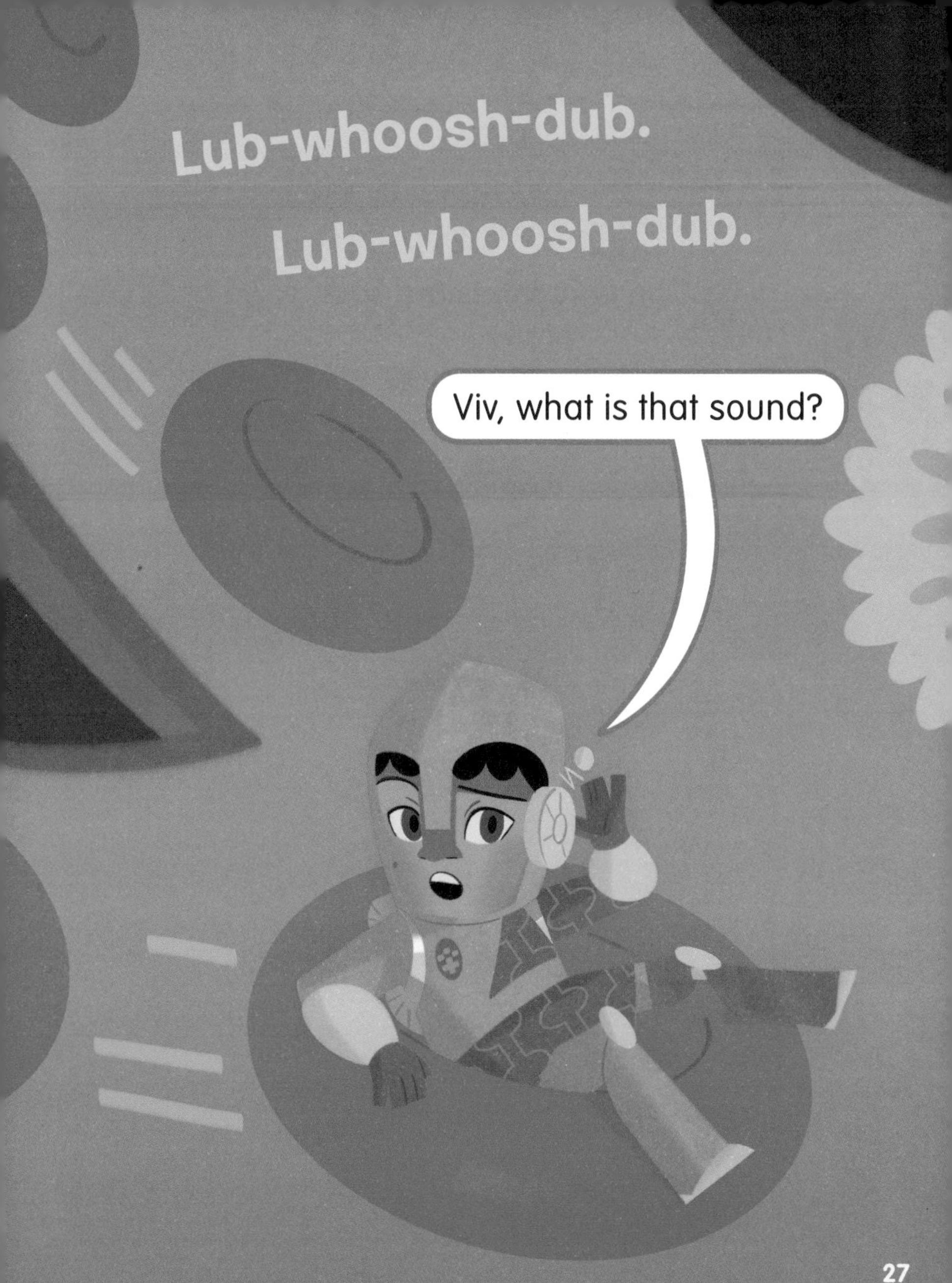
Lub-whoosh-dub.
Lub-whoosh-dub.
Viv, what is that sound?

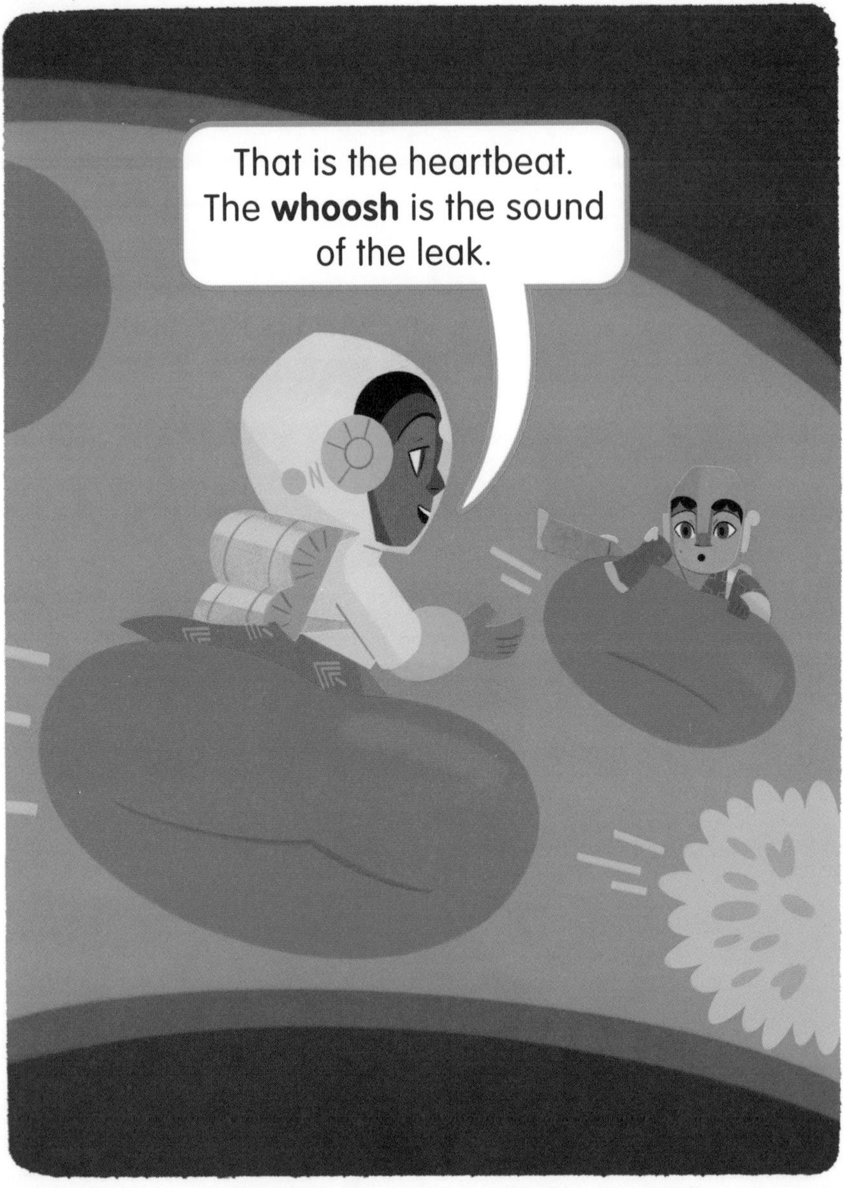
That is the heartbeat. The **whoosh** is the sound of the leak.

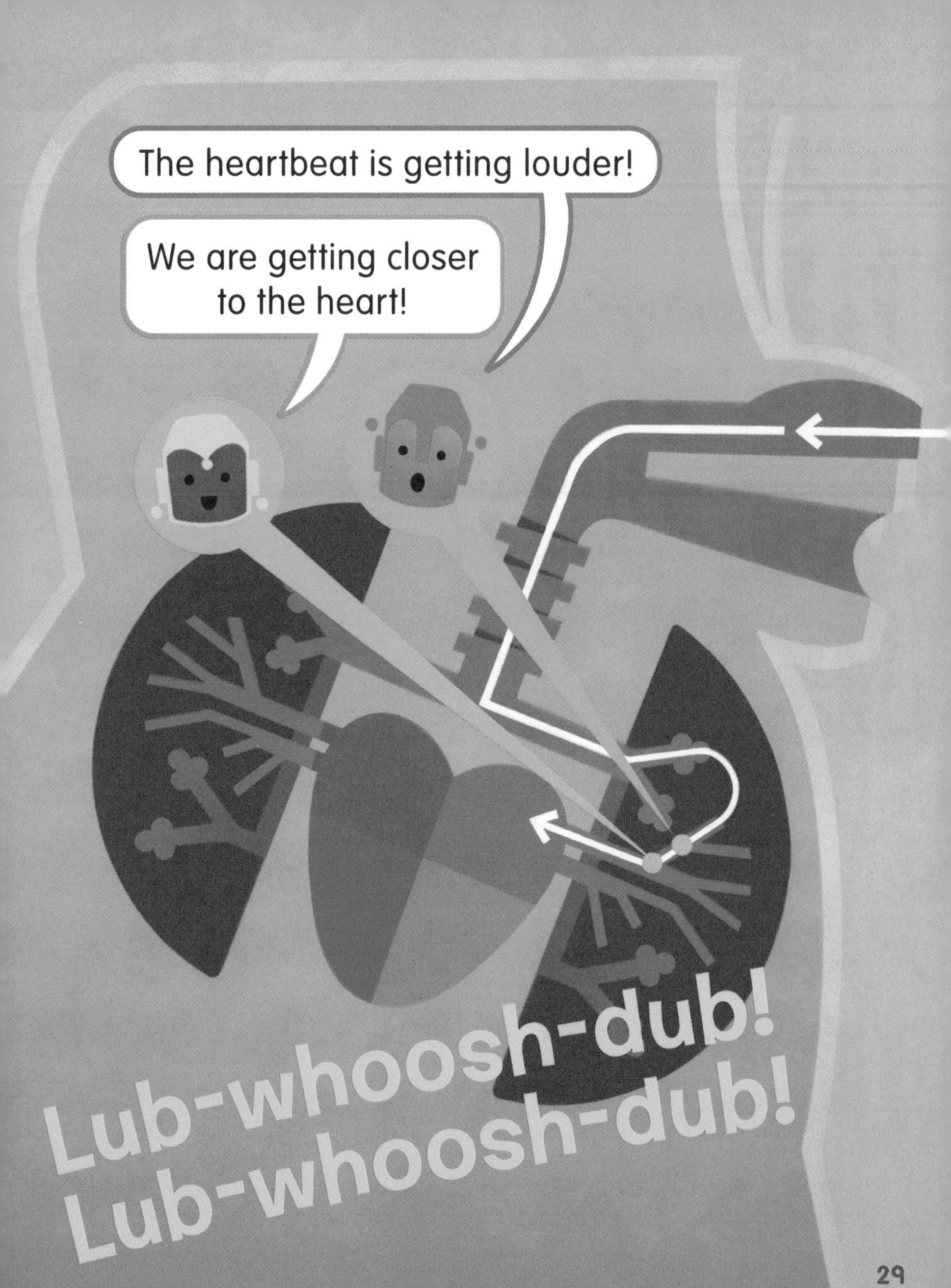
The heartbeat is getting louder!
We are getting closer to the heart!
Lub-whoosh-dub!
Lub-whoosh-dub!

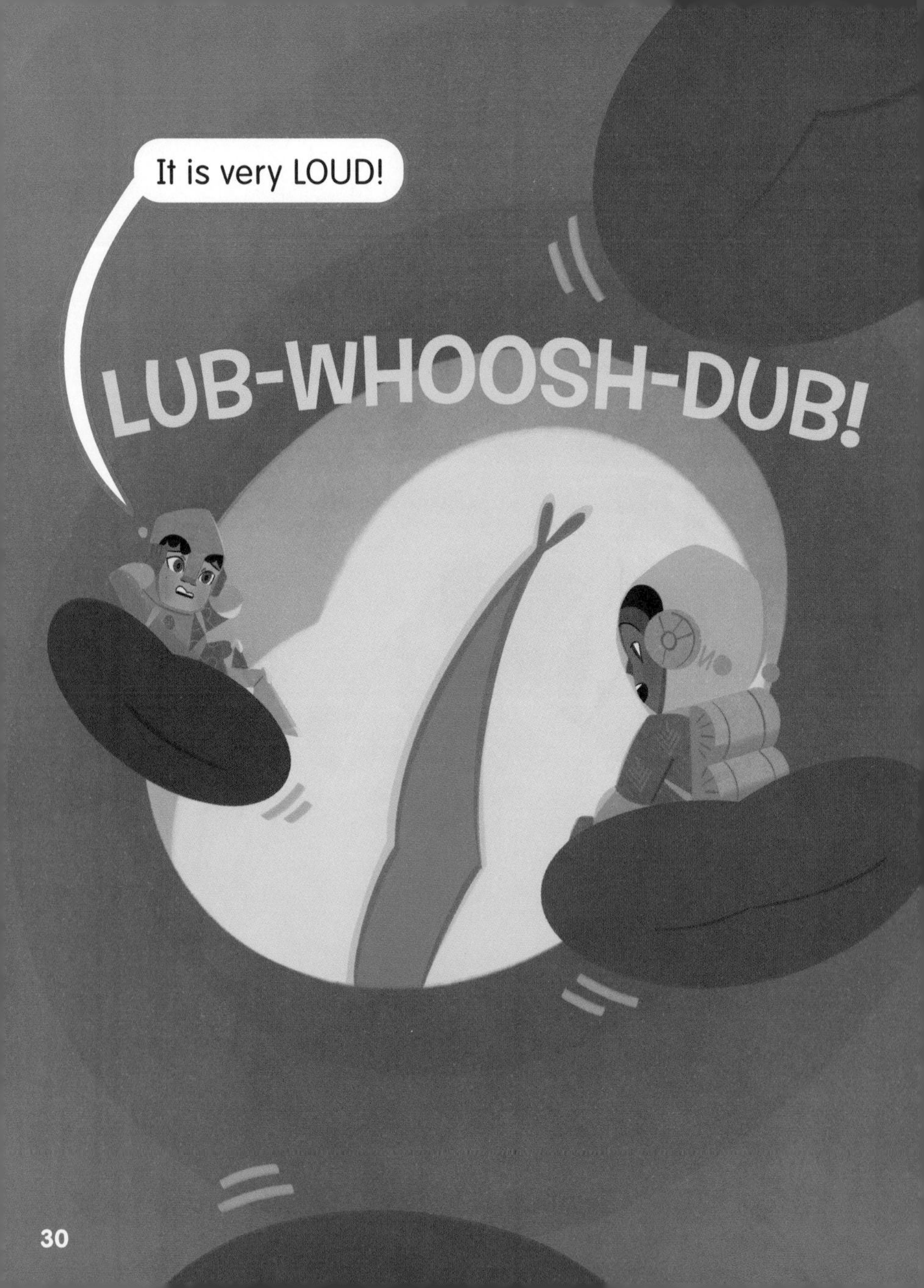
It is very LOUD!
LUB-WHOOSH-DUB!

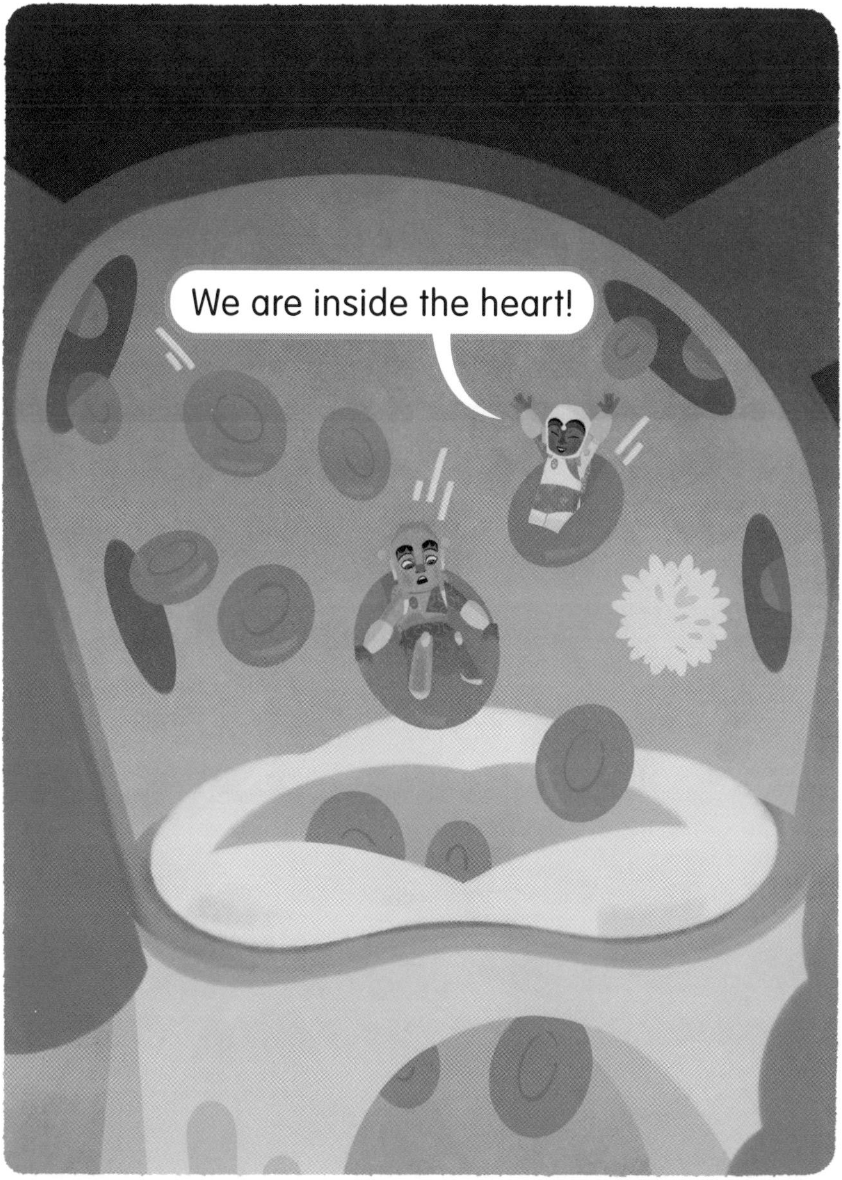
We are inside the heart!

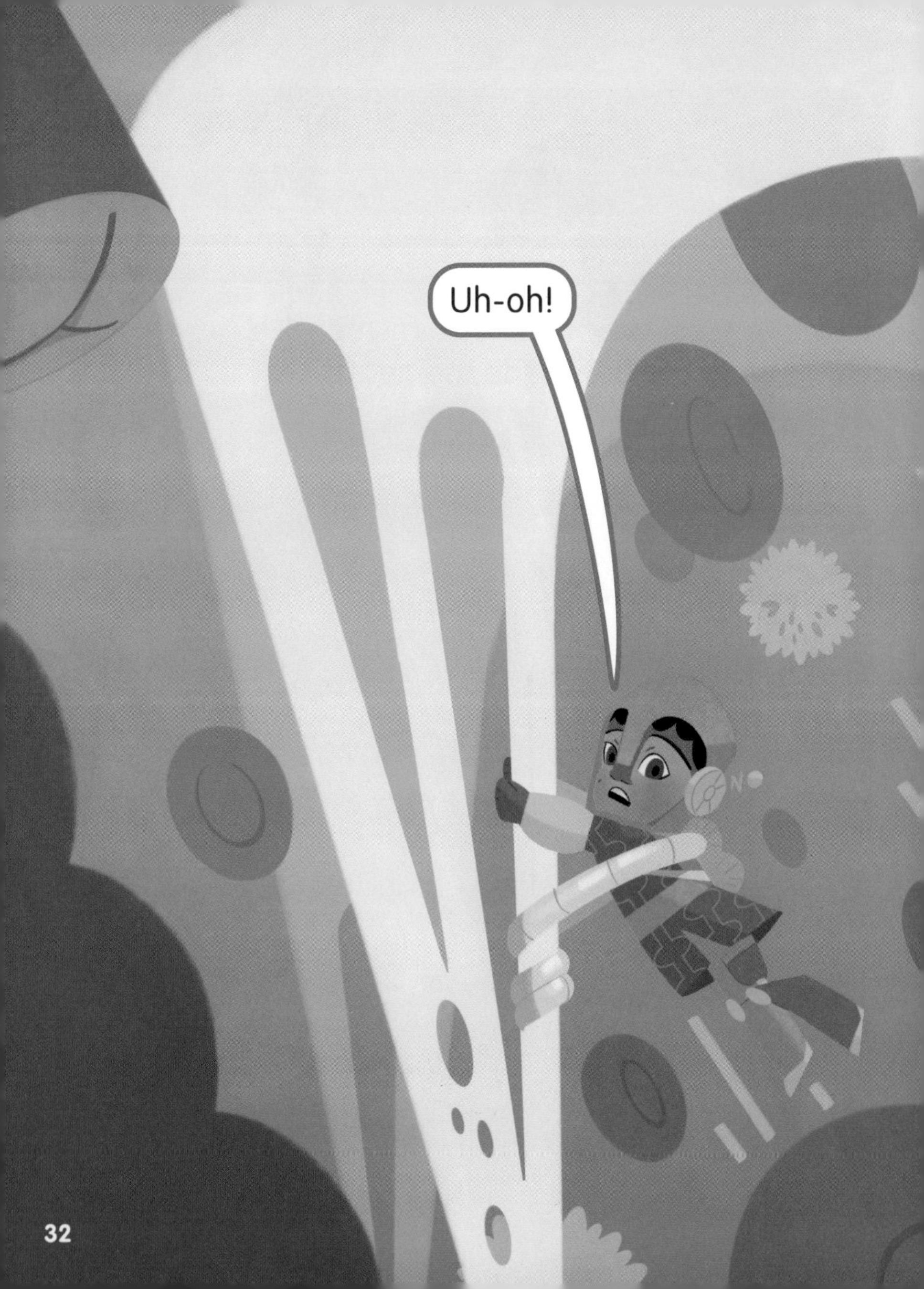
Uh-oh!

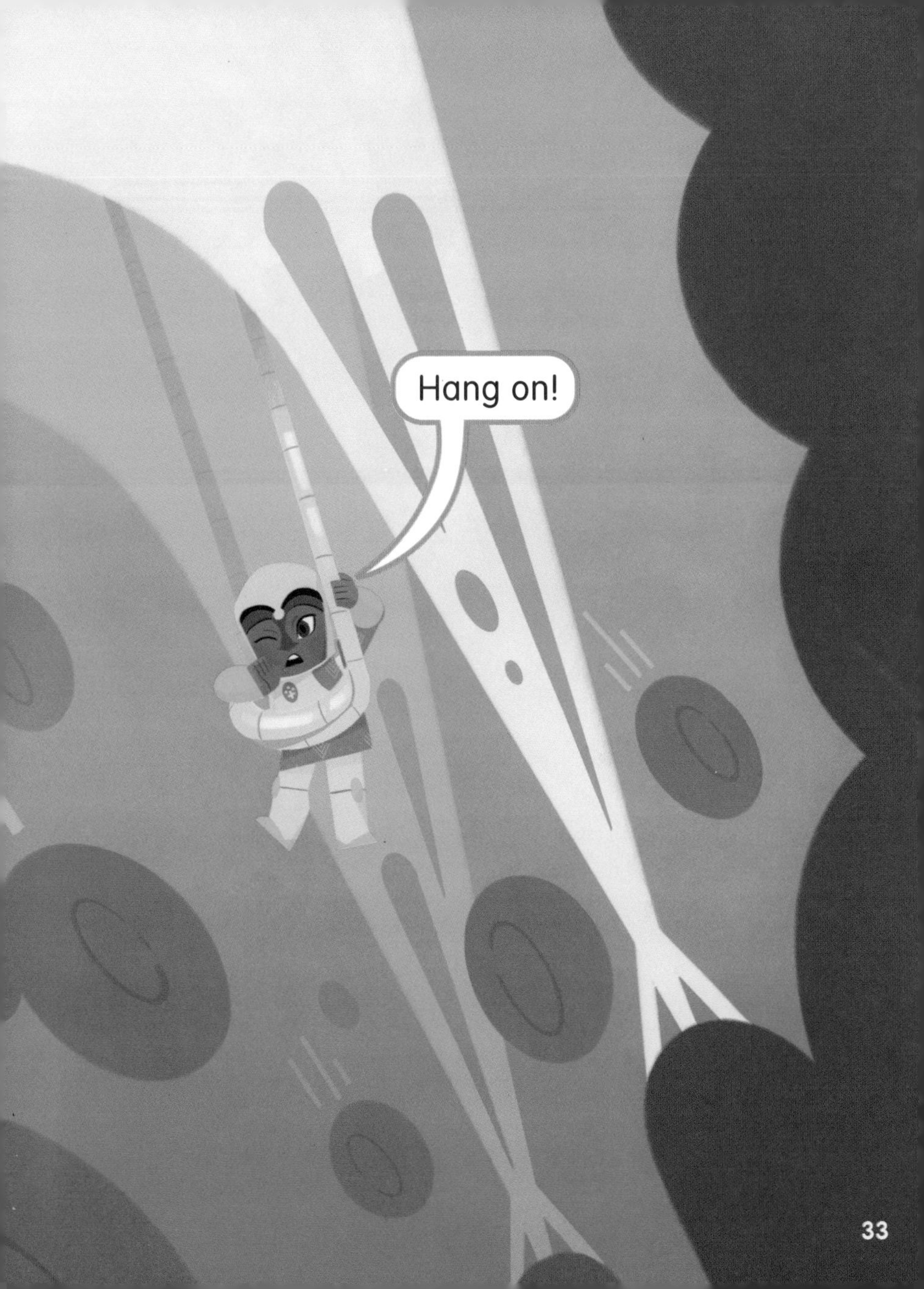
Hang on!

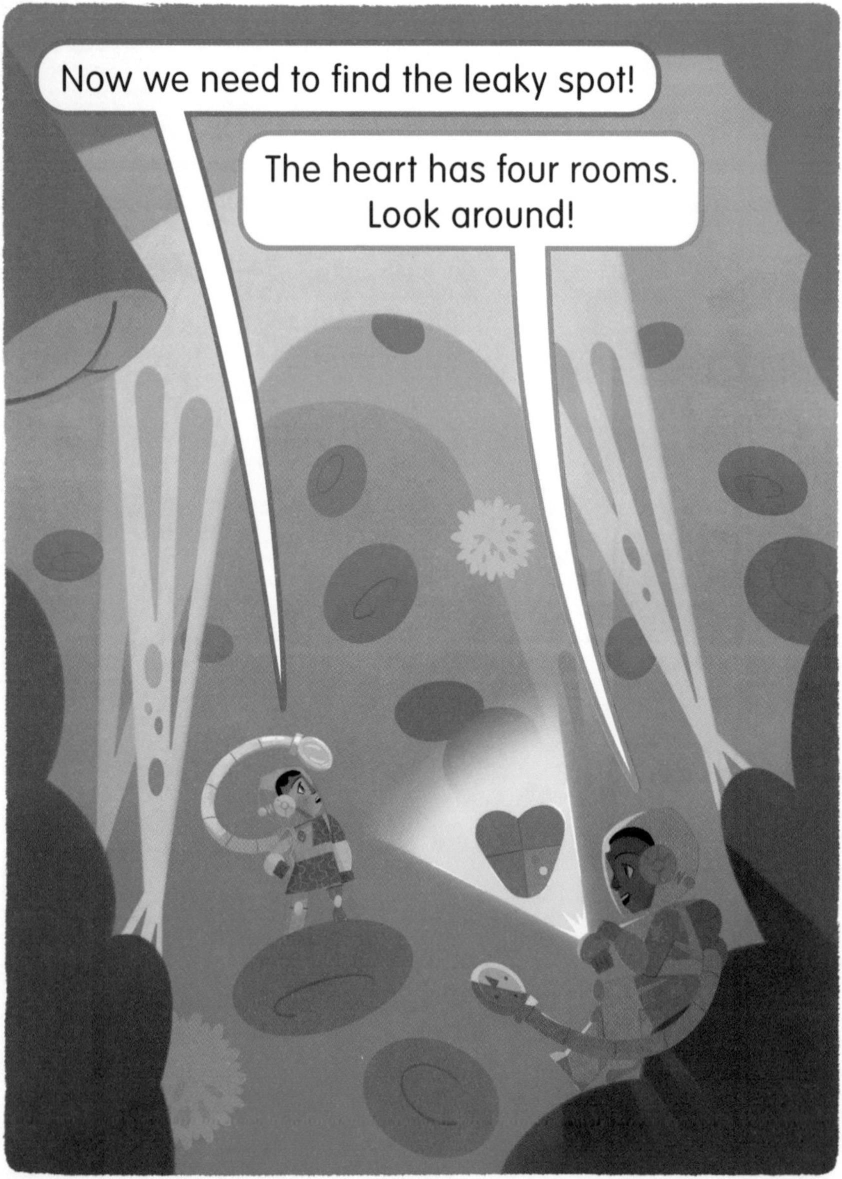
Now we need to find the leaky spot!
The heart has four rooms. Look around!

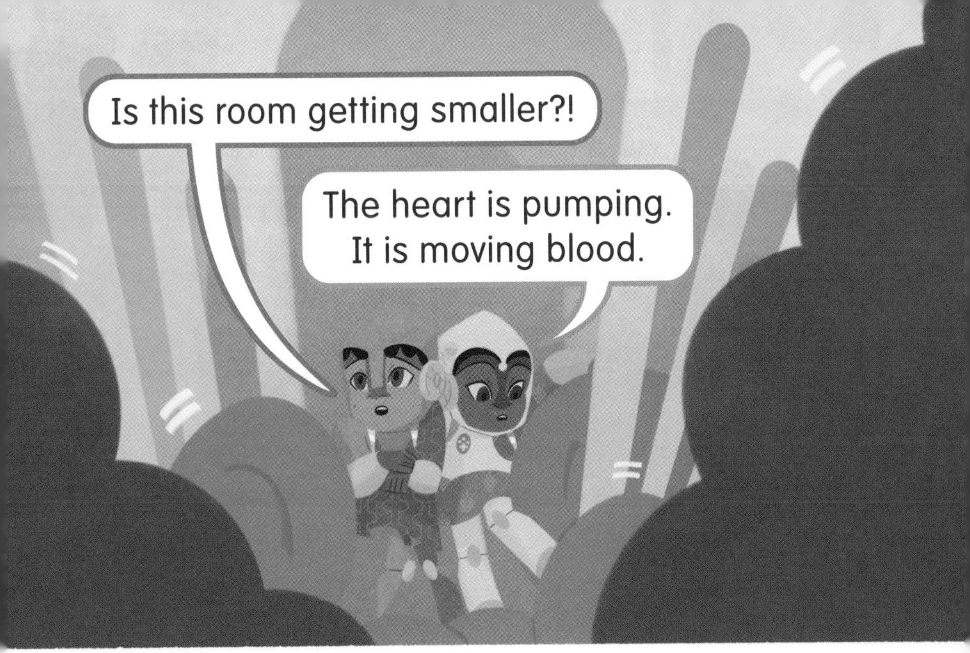
Is this room getting smaller?!
The heart is pumping. It is moving blood.

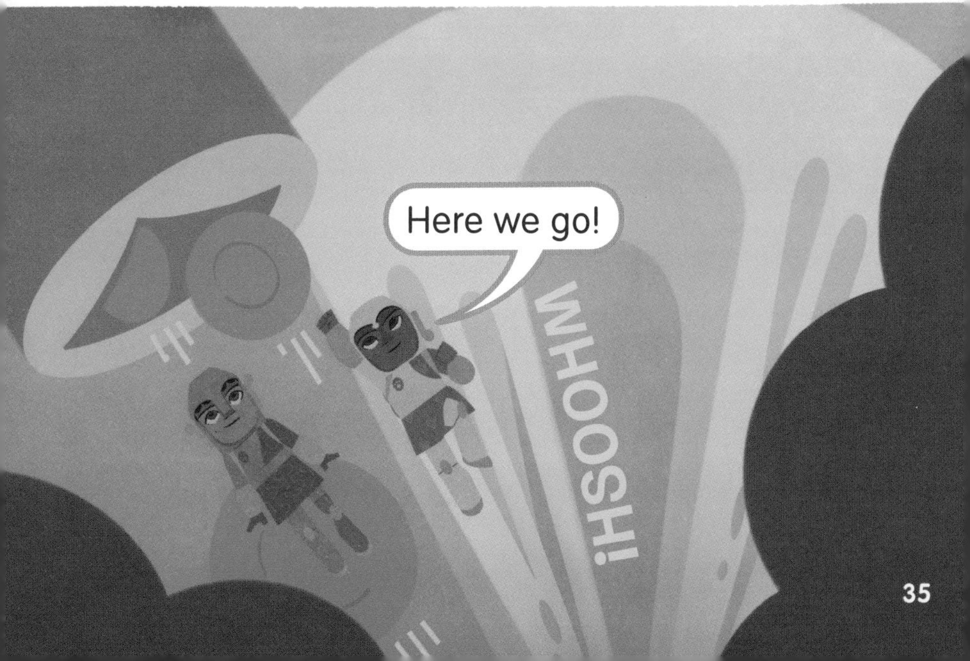
Here we go!
WHOOSH!

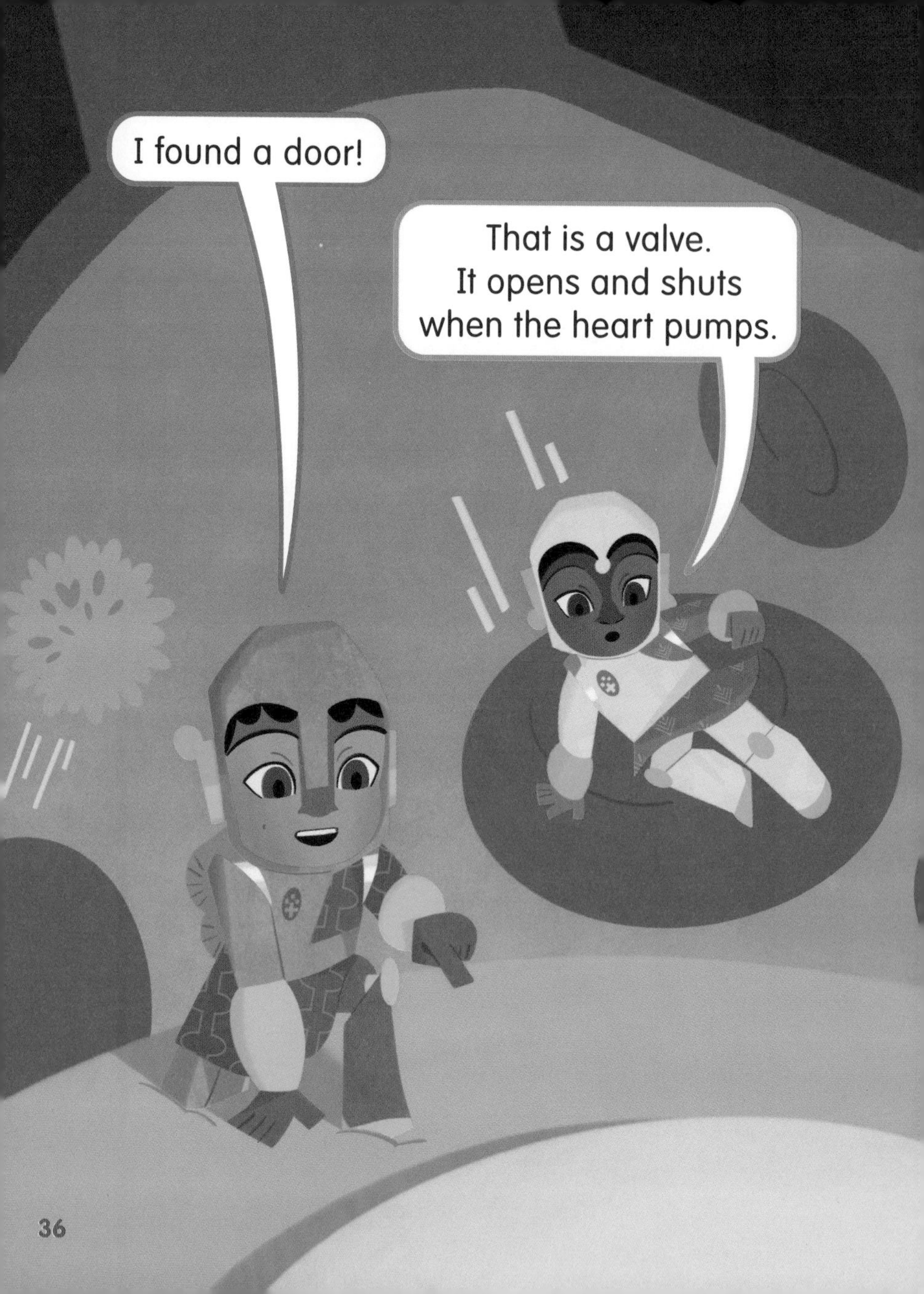
I found a door!
That is a valve. It opens and shuts when the heart pumps.

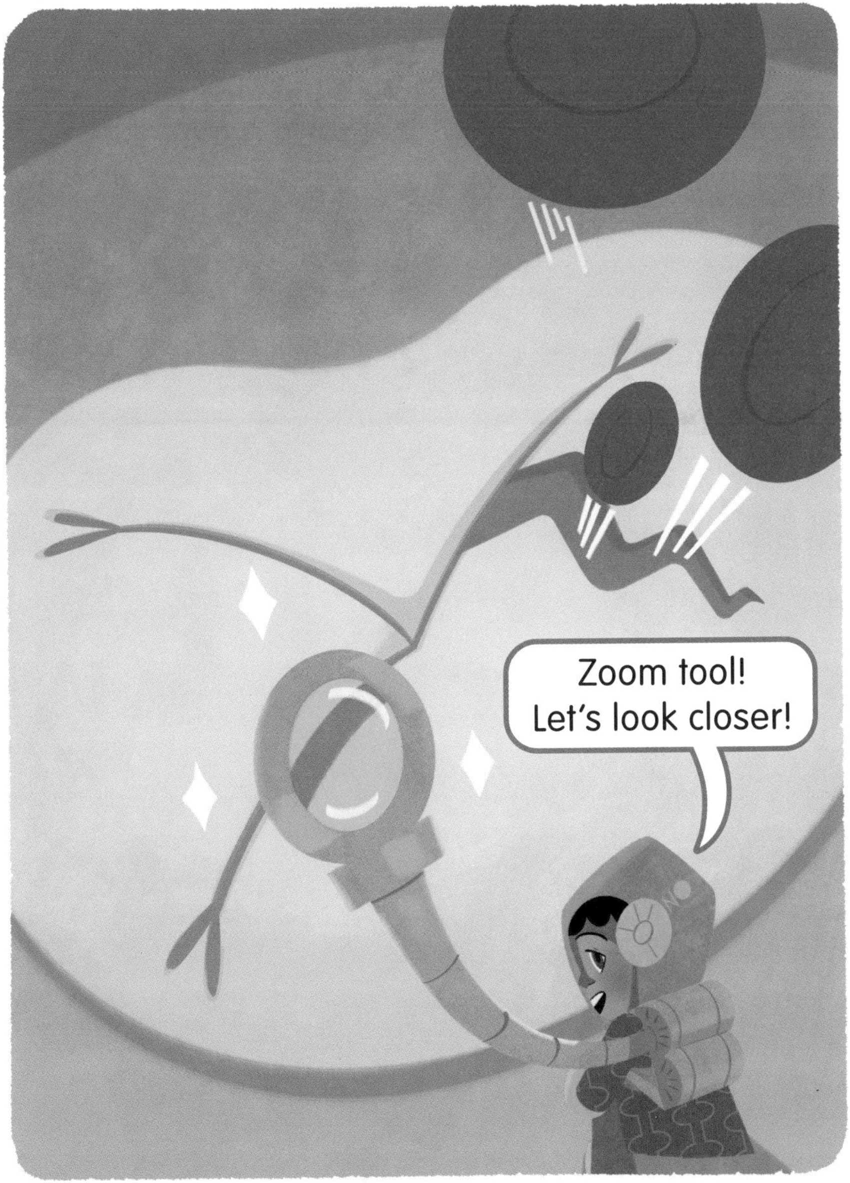
Zoom tool!
Let's look closer!

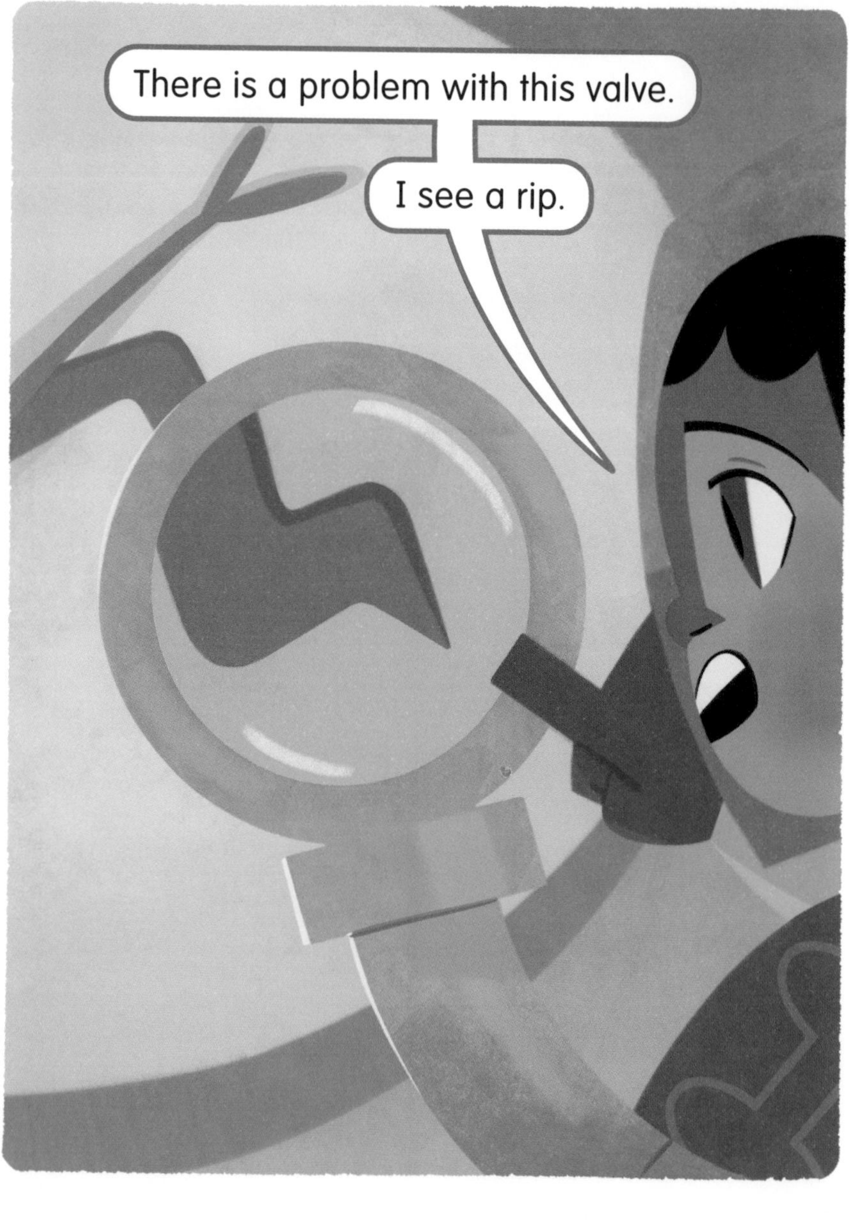
There is a problem with this valve.
I see a rip.

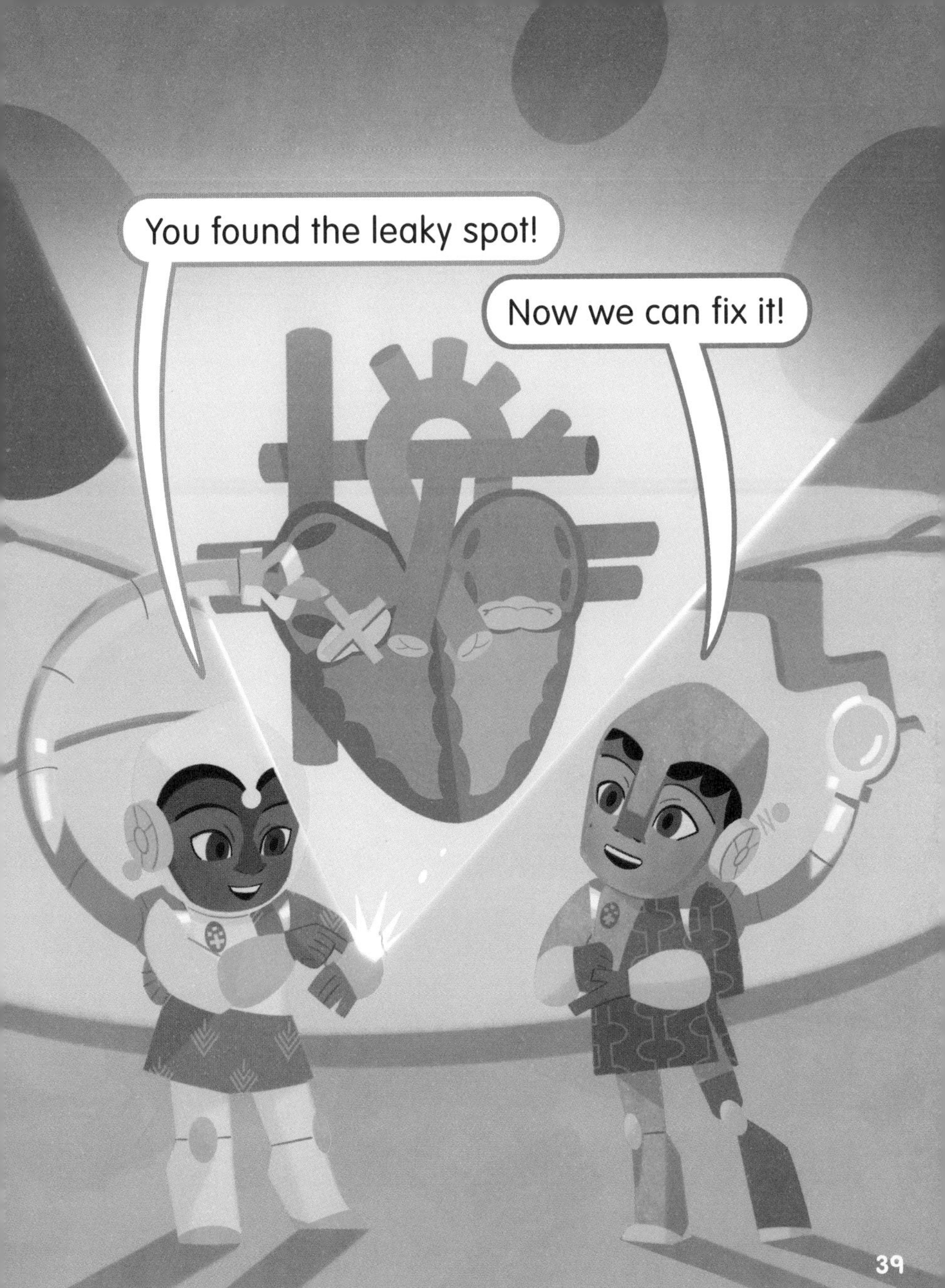
You found the leaky spot!
Now we can fix it!

We Fix the Leak!

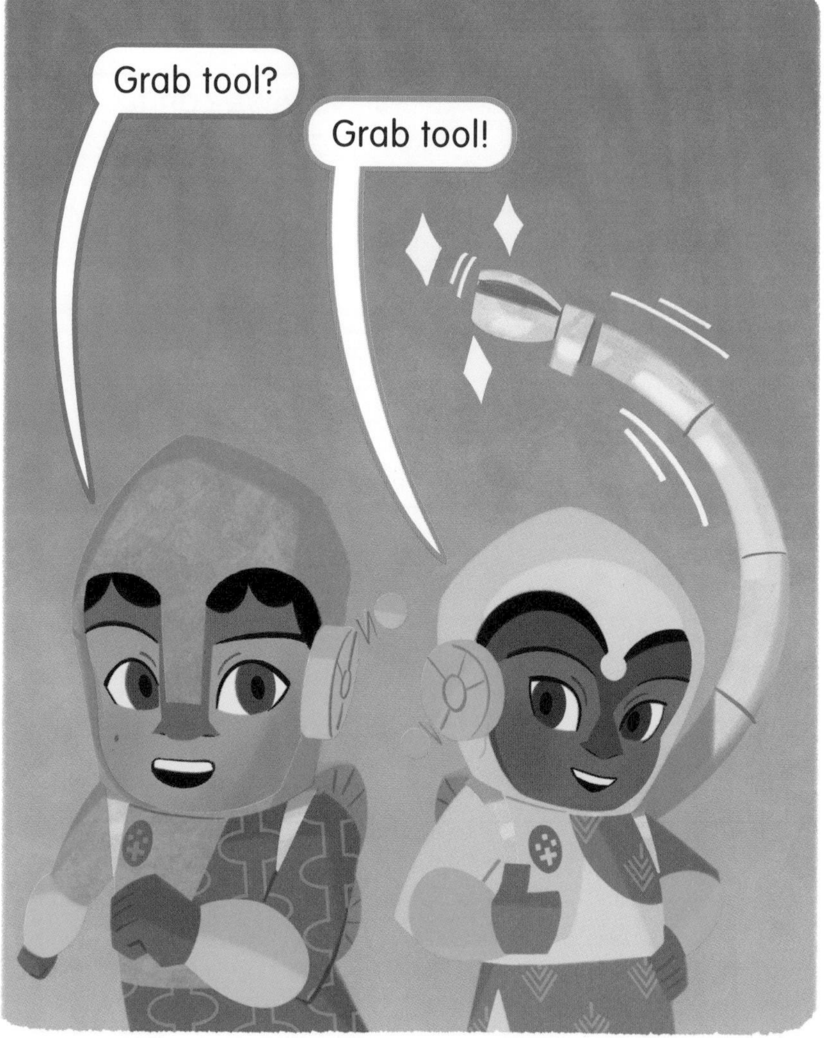

Grab tool?
Grab tool!

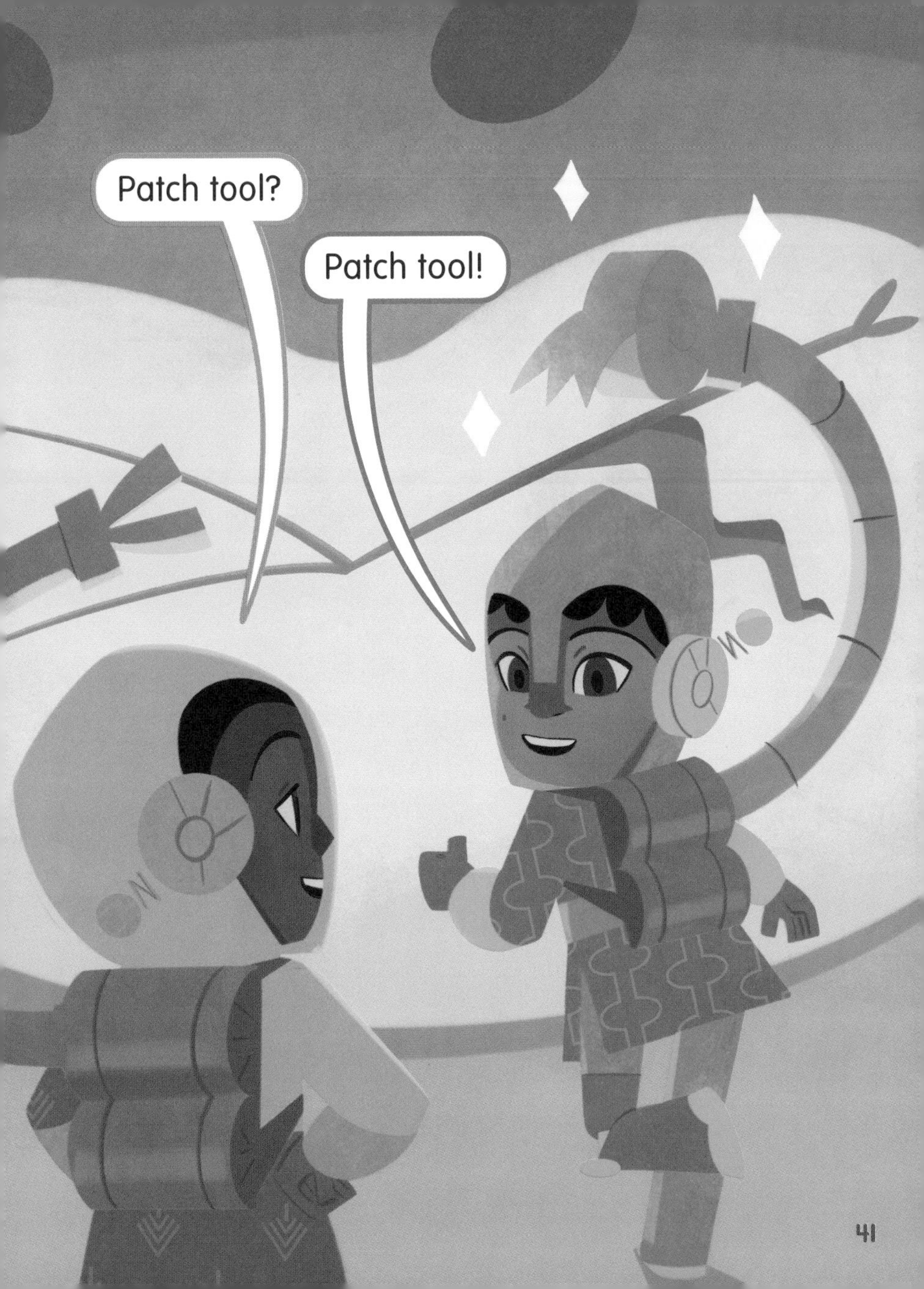
Patch tool?
Patch tool!

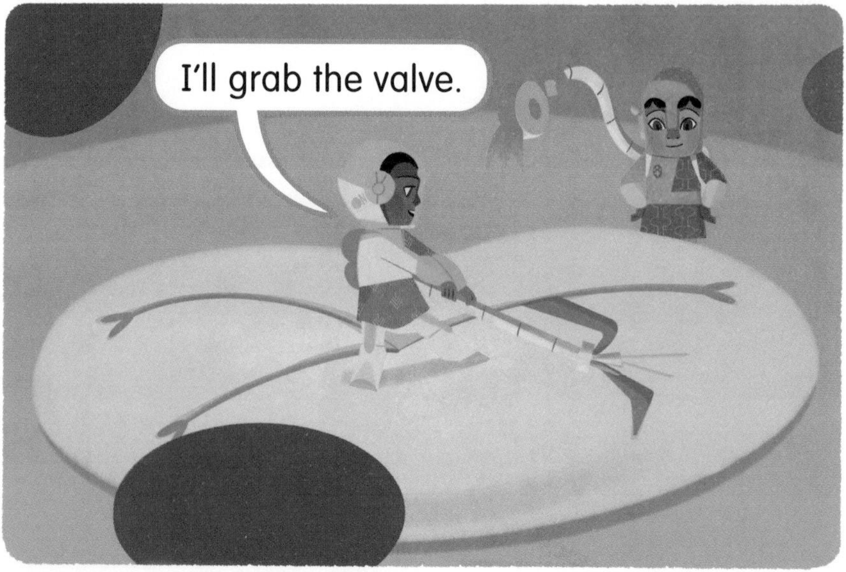
I'll grab the valve.

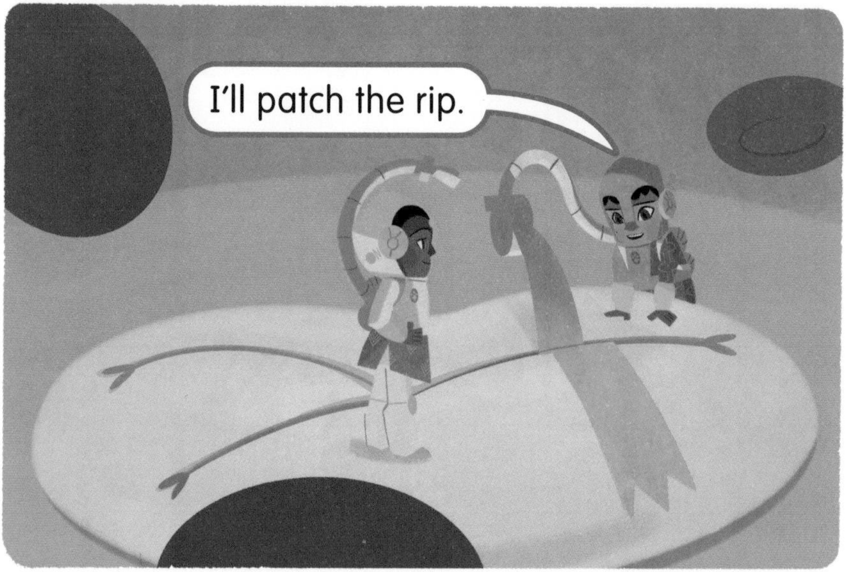
I'll patch the rip.

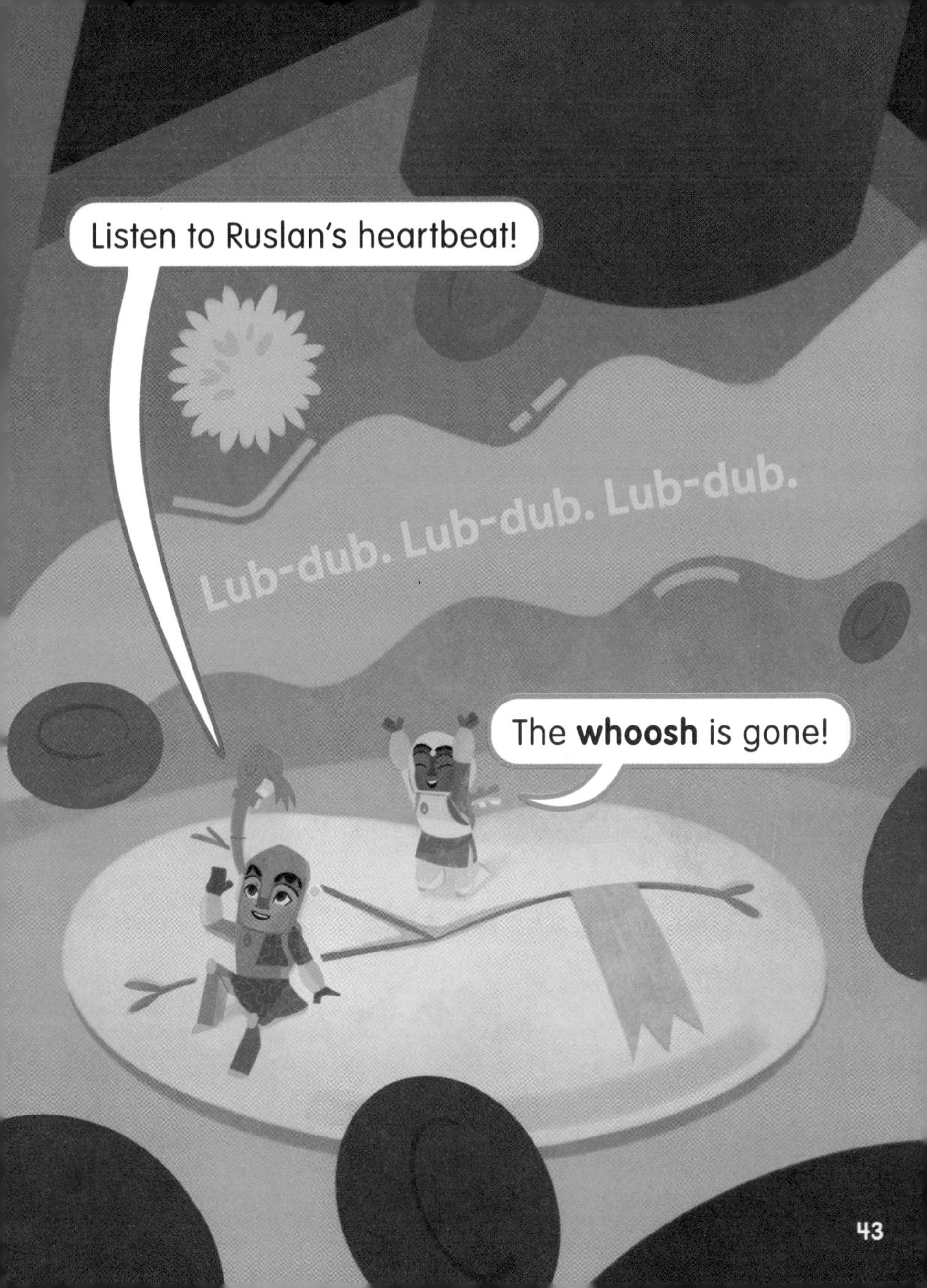
Listen to Ruslan's heartbeat!
Lub-dub. Lub-dub. Lub-dub.
The **whoosh** is gone!

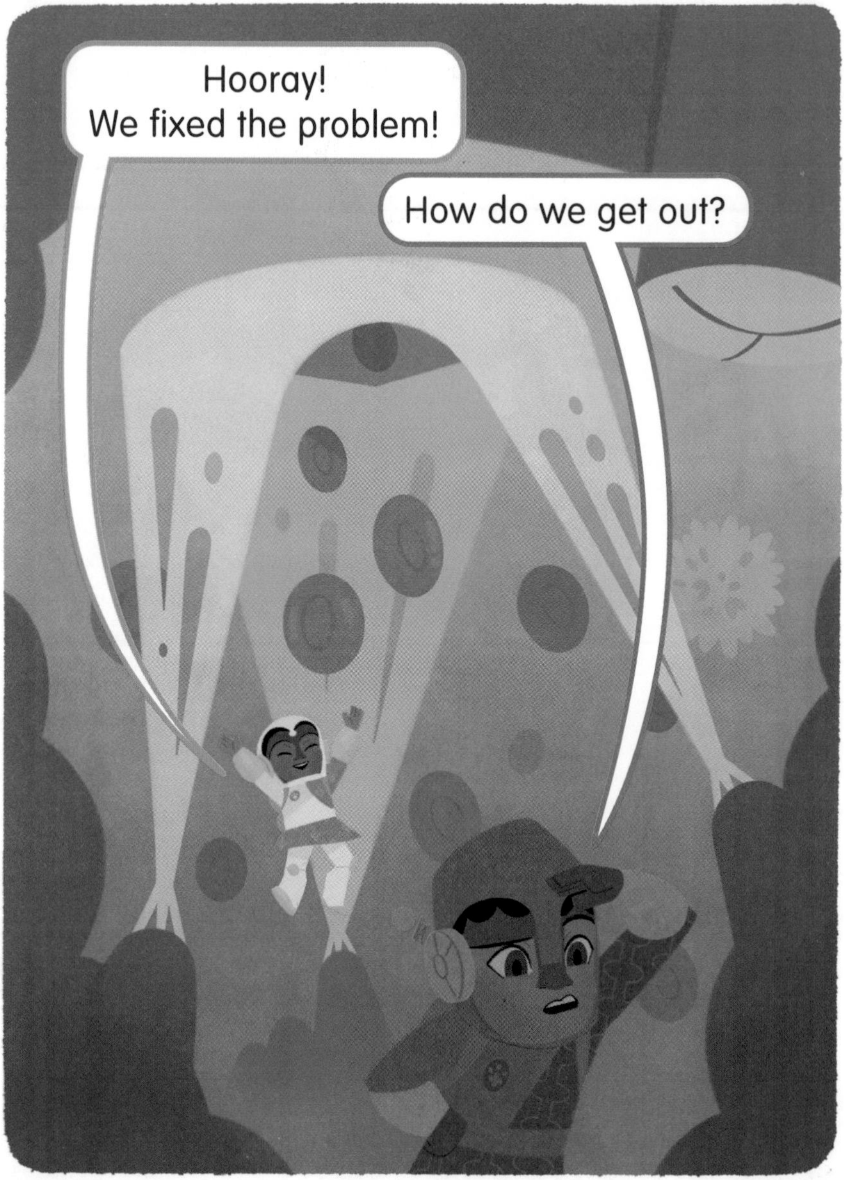
Hooray! We fixed the problem!
How do we get out?

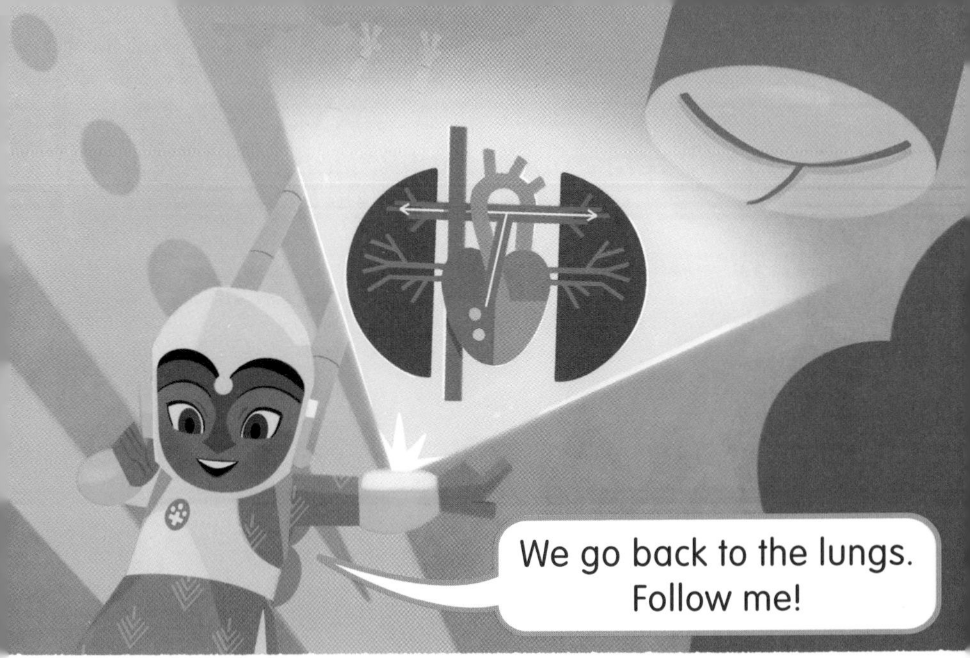
We go back to the lungs.
Follow me!

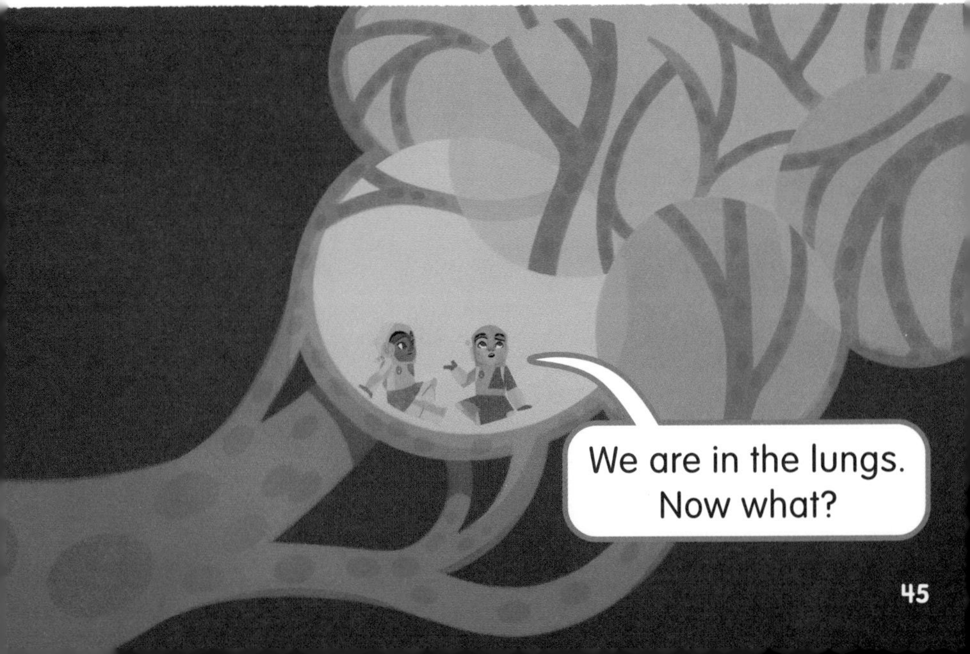
We are in the lungs.
Now what?

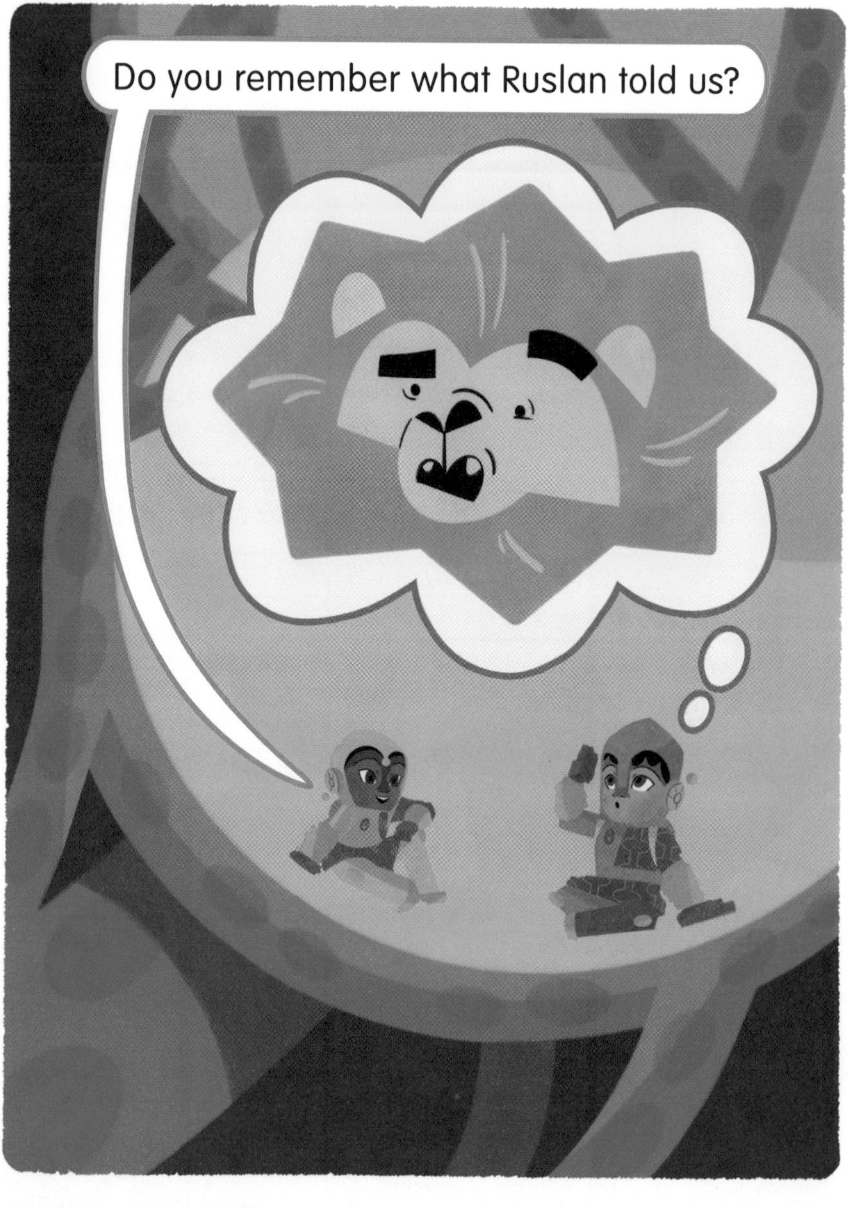
Do you remember what Ruslan told us?

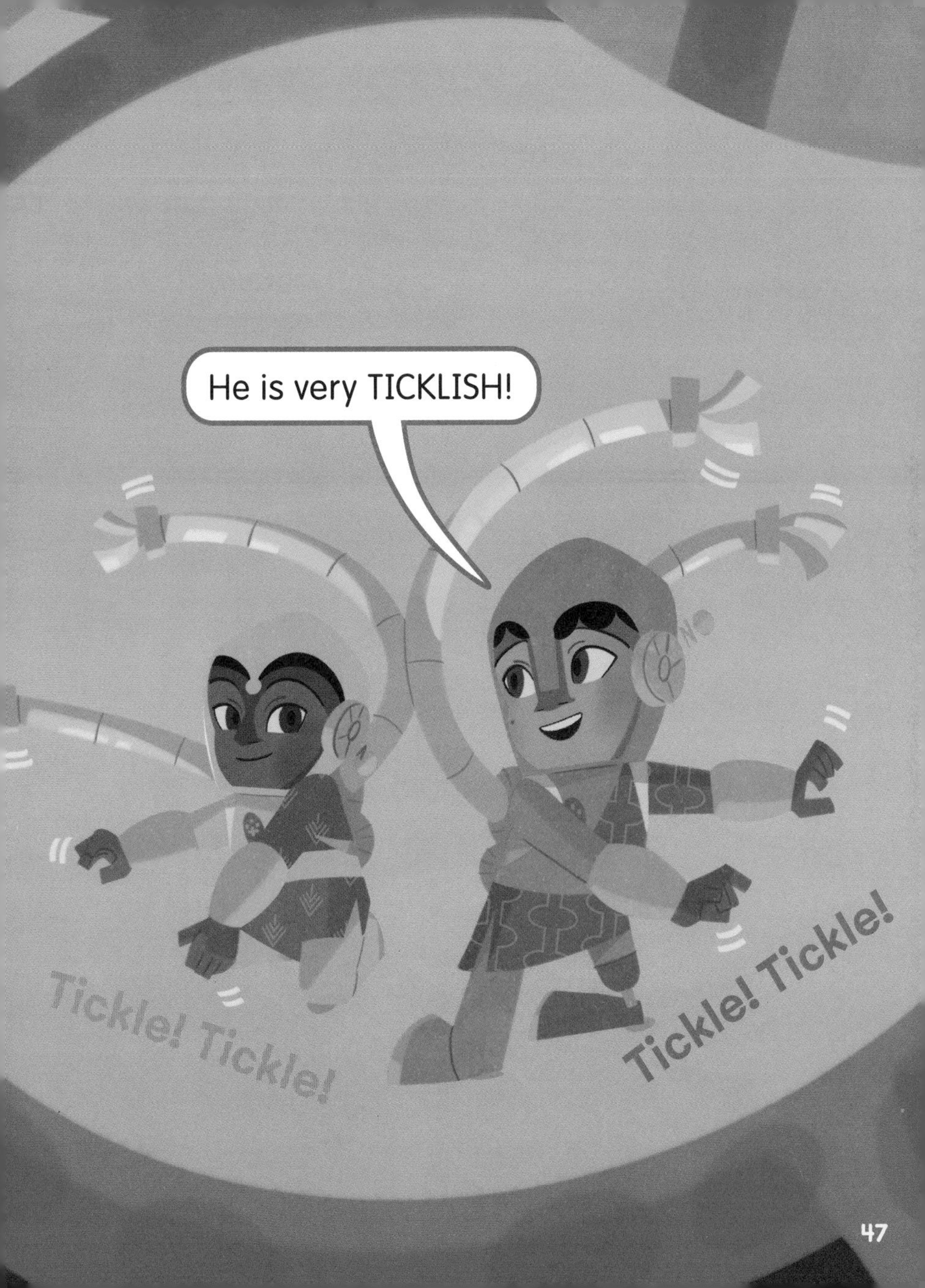
He is very TICKLISH!
Tickle! Tickle!
Tickle! Tickle!

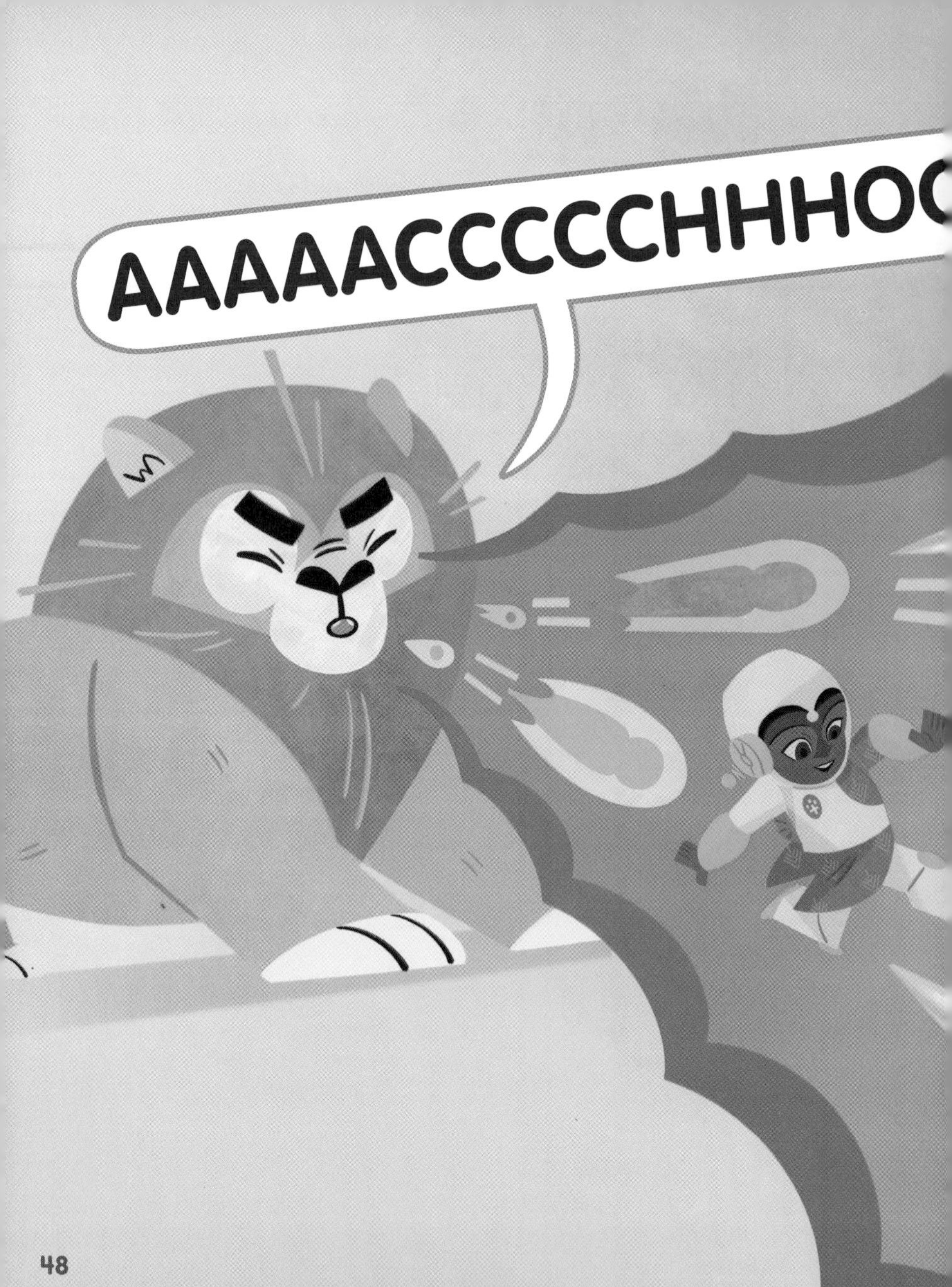
AAAAACCCCCCHHHOO

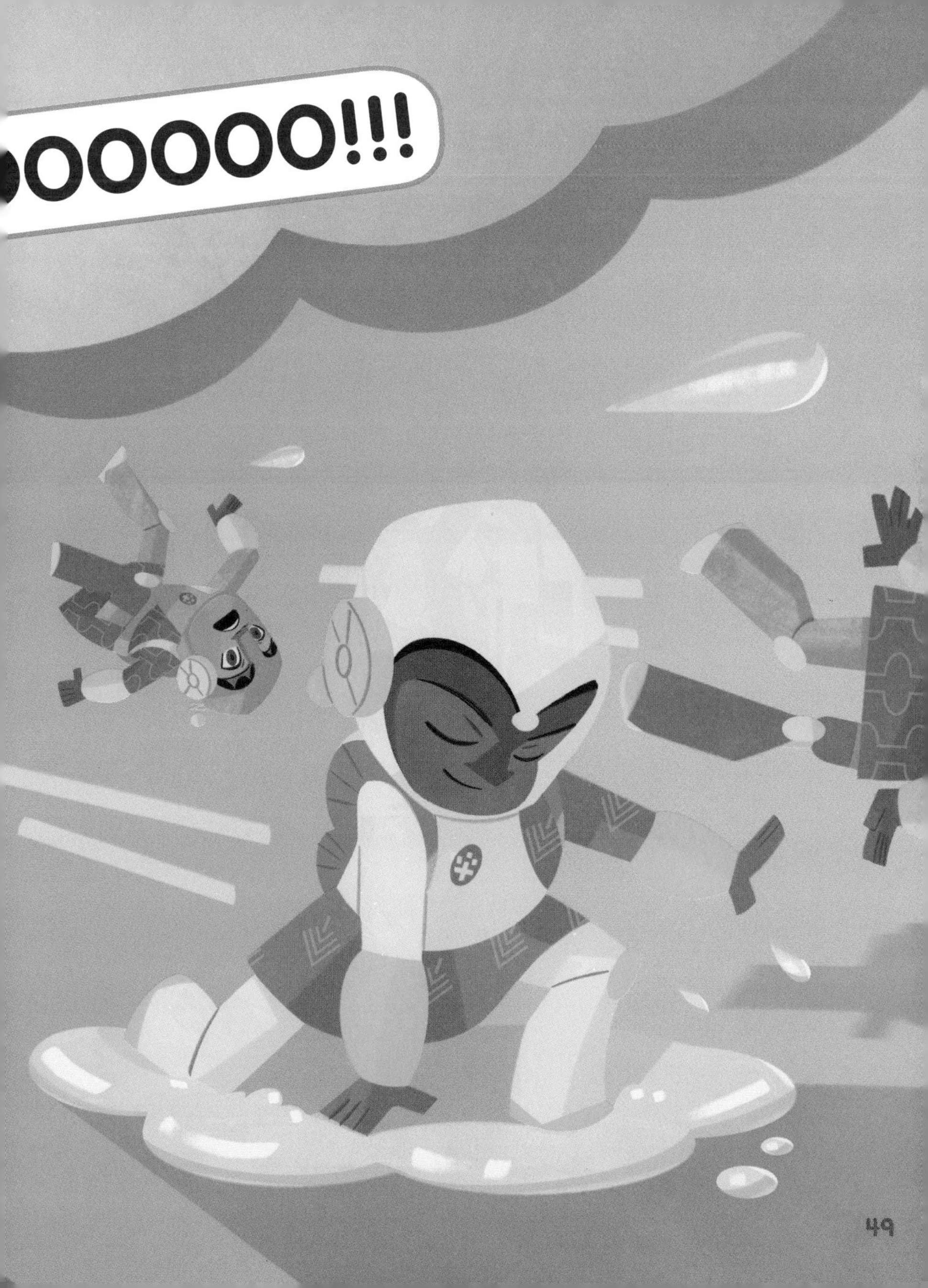
OOOOOO!!!

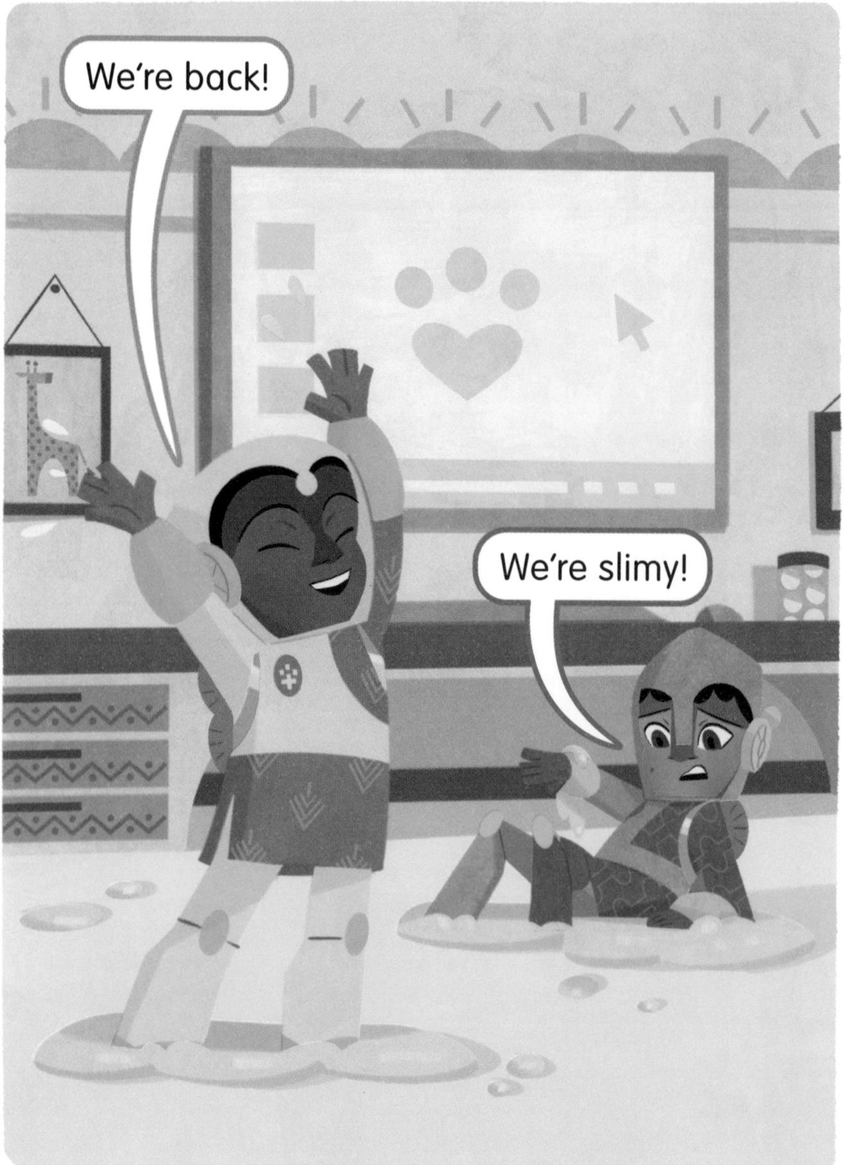
We're back!
We're slimy!

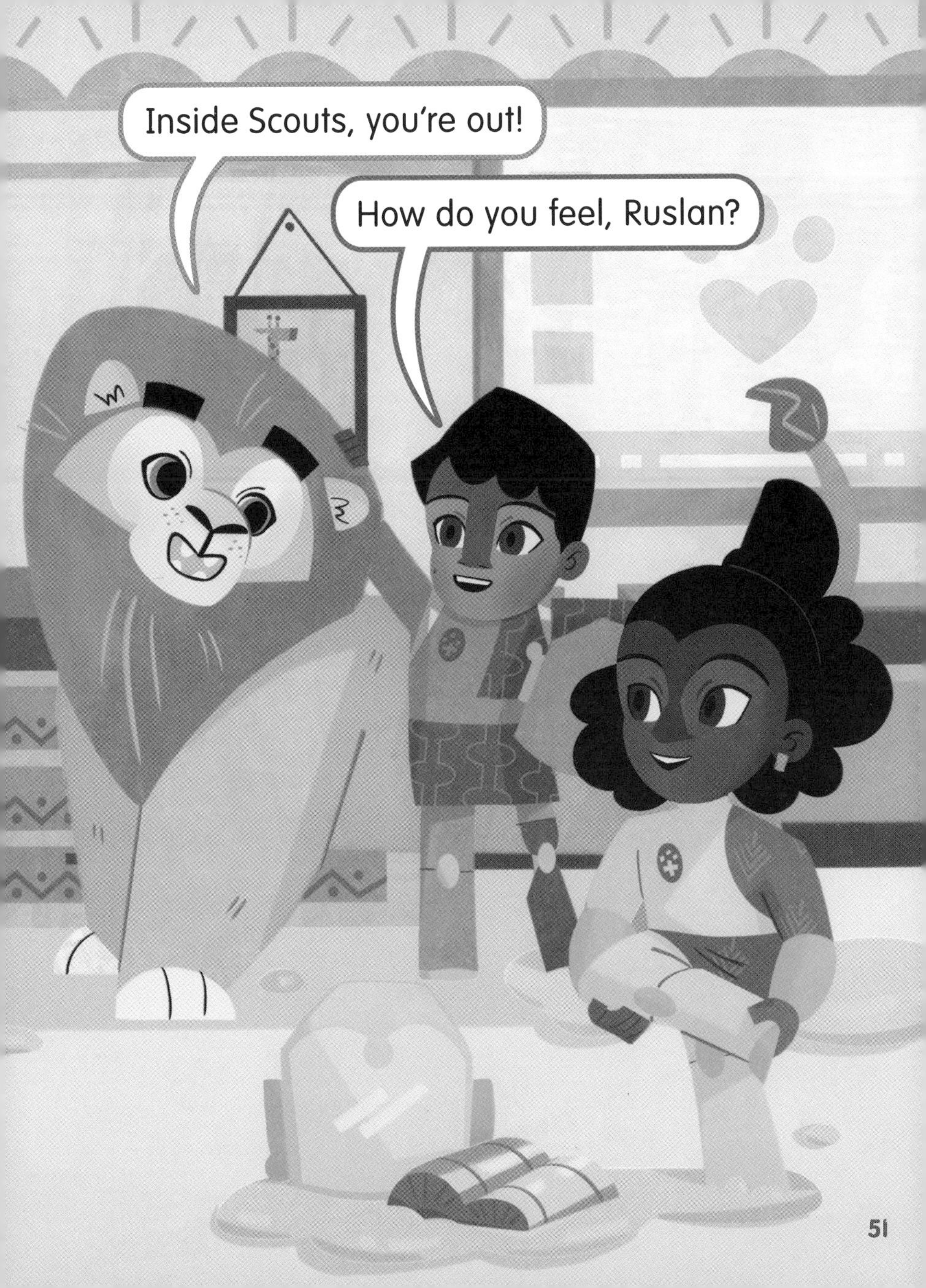
Inside Scouts, you're out!
How do you feel, Ruslan?

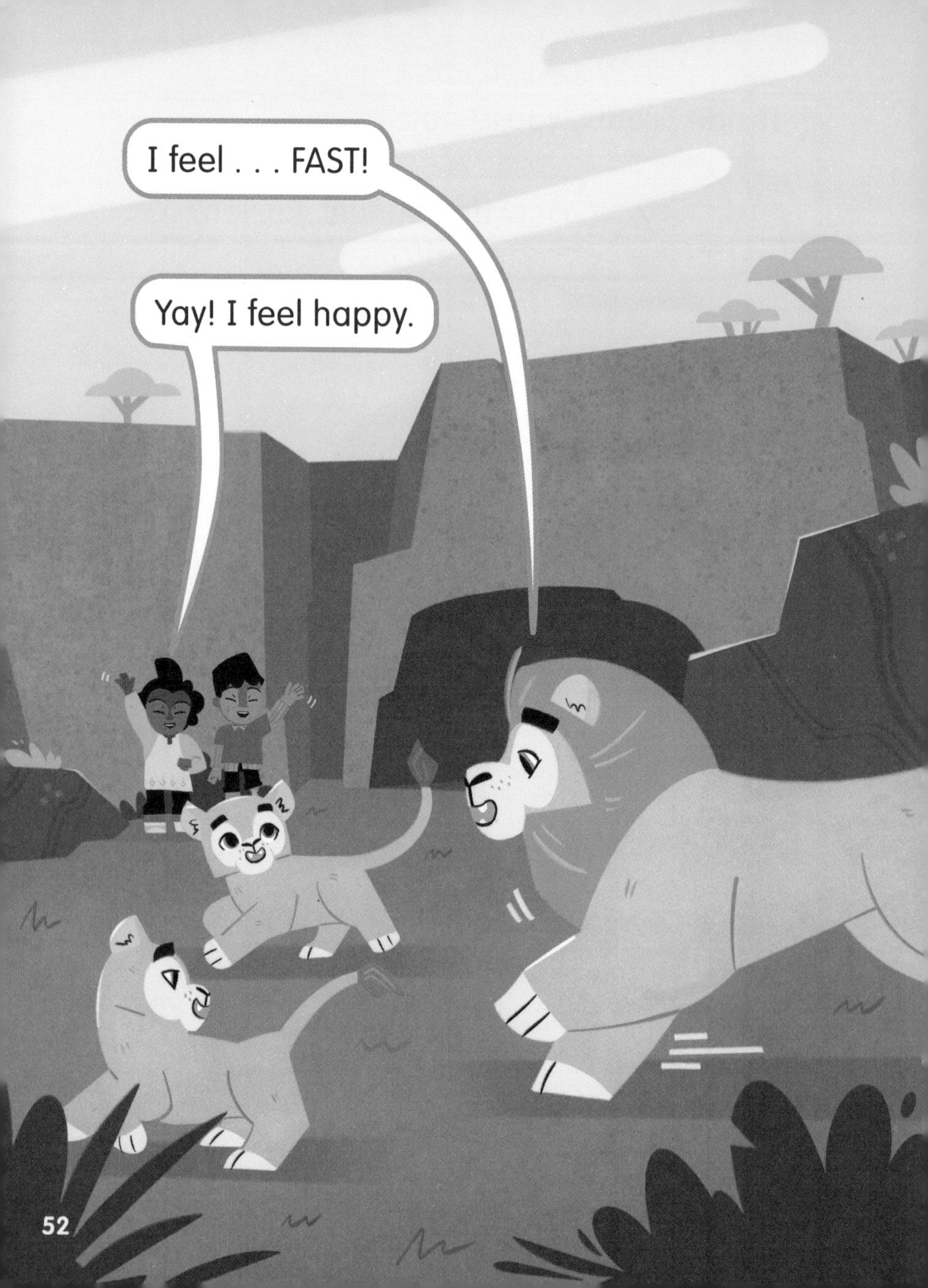
I feel . . . FAST!
Yay! I feel happy.

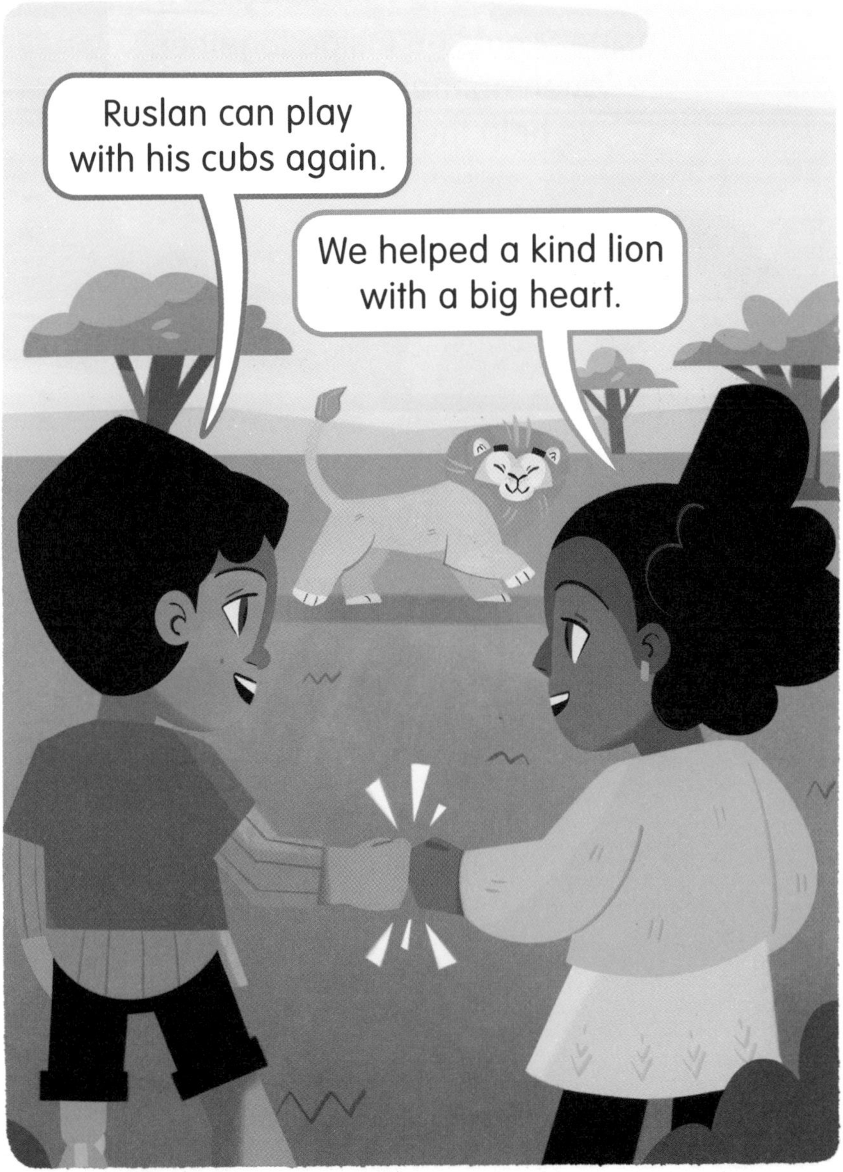
Ruslan can play with his cubs again.
We helped a kind lion with a big heart.

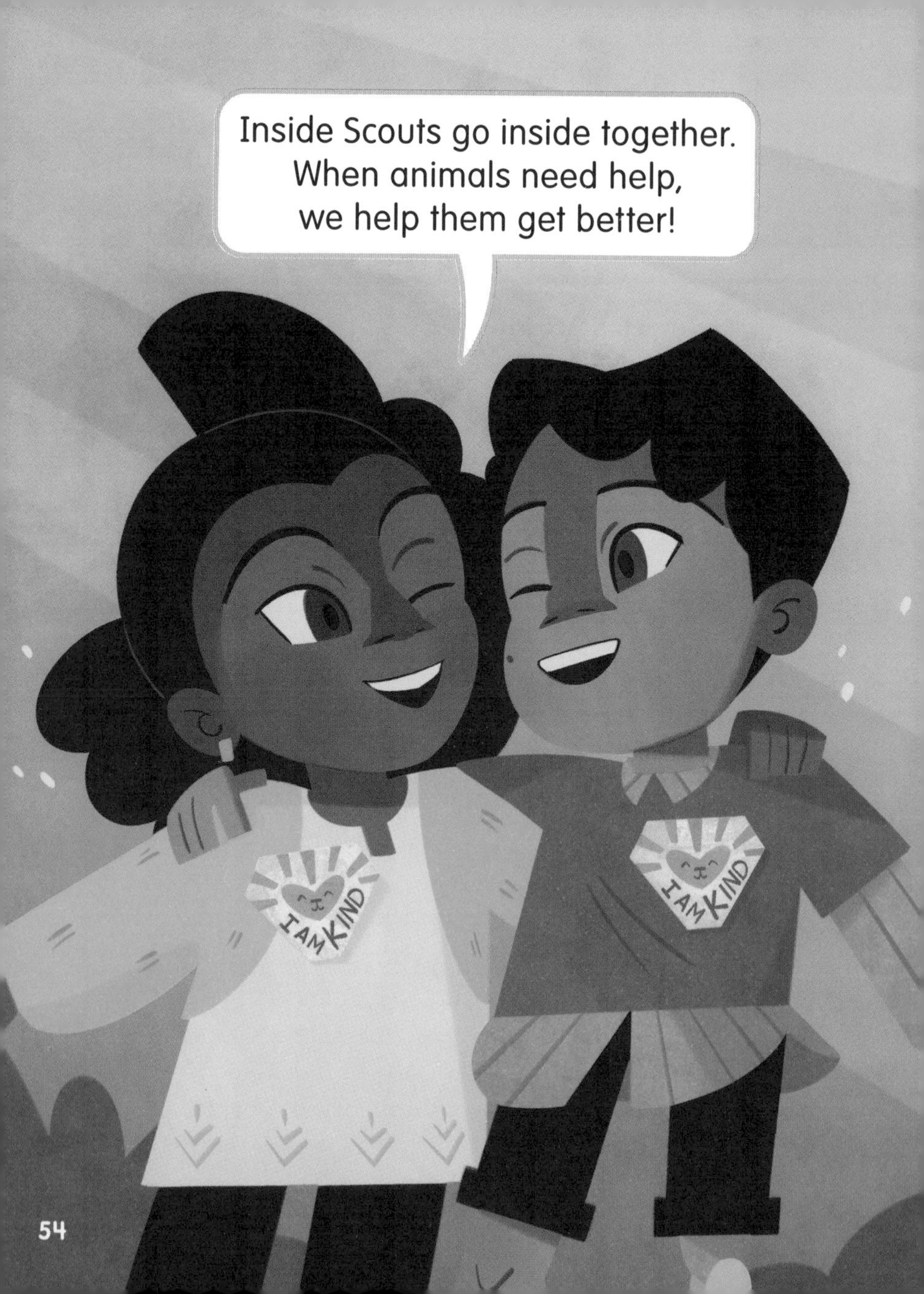
Inside Scouts go inside together.
When animals need help,
we help them get better!
I AM KIND
I AM KIND

About the Creators

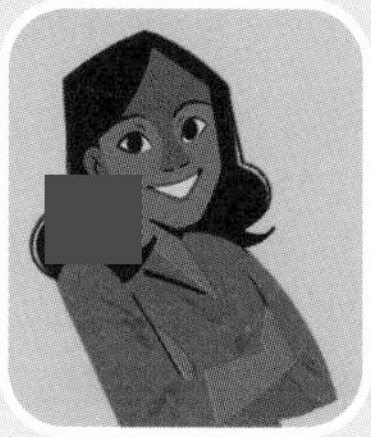

Mitali Banerjee Ruths, MD, was born in New York, grew up in Texas, and now lives in Canada. Before writing books, Mitali studied engineering and medicine.

The idea for The Inside Scouts combines her love for technology, medicine, animals, and the inner workings of our bodies!

The Inside Scouts is Mitali's first early reader series. She is also the author of the early chapter book series The Party Diaries.

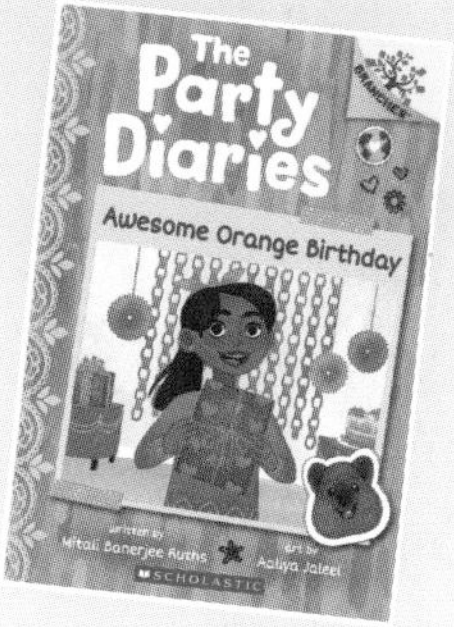
The Party Diaries
Awesome Orange Birthday
Mitali Banerjee Ruths
Aaliya Jaleel
SCHOLASTIC

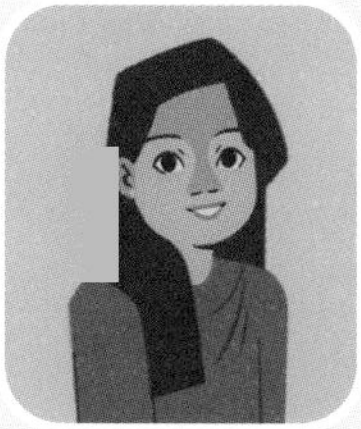

Francesca Mahaney was born and raised in western Massachusetts. She studied illustration in New York City before returning to the quiet woods of New England. Currently, she lives with her three wild cats—Beauregard, Melody, and Sherwin, who also love to run and play.

The Inside Scouts is Francesca's first early reader series.

Fun Facts about the Heart

1. The heart is a pump that moves, or **circulates**, blood around the body. It is part of the **circulatory** (SUR-kyuh-luh-tor-ee) system.

LUNG
HEART
LUNG

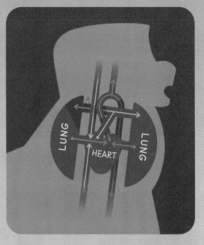

2. The heart pumps blood through tubes called **arteries** (AHR-tur-eez). Then blood returns to the heart through tubes called **veins** (vaynz). Arteries move blood away from the heart. Veins move blood back to the heart.

HEART
VEINS
ARTERIES
BODY

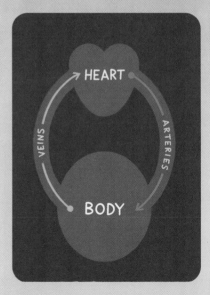

3 Lions, humans, and other mammals have hearts with four **chambers**, or rooms.
© = chamber

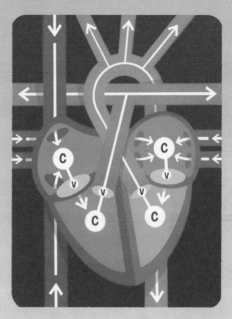

4 Mammal hearts have four **valves**, or doors. Valves open and close to keep blood flowing the right way through the heart.
ⓥ = valve

5 Healthy hearts make a **lub-dub** sound with every heartbeat. This sound comes from the valves closing.

DRAW YOUR OWN "I AM KIND" BADGE!

1 Draw a triangle without the corners.

2 Connect the lines to make a closed shape.

3 Draw a heart in the middle of the shape.

4 Draw a happy face inside the heart.

5 Write "I AM KIND" below the heart. Then add lines coming out from the top of the heart.

6 Color in your drawing!

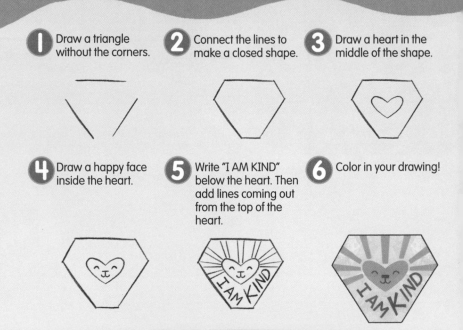

WHAT'S YOUR STORY?

Being kind means thinking of ways to make someone else's day a little better. You can be kind with what you say, what you do, and how you treat others. How can **you** make someone else's day better? Write and draw your story! Then go do your kind action!